What if...
All Your Dreams
Came True

a choose
your destiny
NOVEL

What if...
All Your Dreams
Came True

LIZ RUCKDESCHEL AND SARA JAMES

DELACORTE PRESS

All rights reserved. Published in the United States by Delacorte Press, an imprint of Random House Children's Books, a division of Random House, Inc., New York.

Delacorte Press is a registered trademark and the colophon is a trademark of Random House, Inc.

Visit us on the Web! www.randomhouse.com/teens

Educators and librarians, for a variety of teaching tools, visit us at www.randomhouse.com/teachers

Library of Congress Cataloging-in-Publication Data
Ruckdeschel, Liz
What if—all your dreams came true / Liz Ruckdeschel and Sara James.
— 1st trade paperback ed.
p. cm.
Summary: As Haley's junior year at Hillsdale High comes to a close, the reader helps her to make decisions about prom and other activities, as well as what to do during the summer to prepare for her all-important senior year and the rest of her life.
ISBN 978-0-385-73819-4 (trade pbk.) ISBN 978-0-375-89340-7 (e-book)
1. Plot-your-own stories. [1. Popularity—Fiction. 2. High schools—Fiction. 3. Schools—Fiction. 4. Plot-your-own stories.]
I. James, Sara. II. Title.
PZ7.R842Wgy 2009
[Fic]—dc22
2009014628

Printed in the United States of America

10 9 8 7 6 5 4 3 2 1

First Edition

What if...
All Your Dreams
Came True

Nothing grows without roots.

"Isn't it supposed to be spring?" Haley Miller complained. She sat in her kitchen on a dreary March morning, ignoring a bowl of oatmeal and watching a light, wet snow fall on the dead leaves in the backyard. "Spring break's over. Winter officially ended last week. It's time for sun."

"These East Coast winters do seem to last forever," said her mother, Joan, sipping a cup of tea. "It's not like spring in Marin, that's for sure."

This was Haley's second New Jersey spring, and

she was still adjusting to the disappointing weather. The Millers had moved to Hillsdale from Marin County in Northern California, where all year round the trees bloomed, the sun nestled like a poached egg in a brilliant blue sky and a mild breeze puffed off the Pacific Ocean. Nothing like the melting slush and gunmetal gray skies of Jersey.

Haley's little brother, Mitchell, licked yogurt off his pudgy fingers, then tugged on Haley's straight auburn hair. It was one of his ways of getting her attention. The attention this usually got from her, however, was negative.

"Mitchell, stop it." Haley swatted his fingers away. "What is it with you and my hair?"

Mitchell responded by tugging on her hair again. Over the years he'd gotten strained peas, a lollipop and several chunks of chewing gum in her hair. She didn't appreciate it.

"What?" Haley snapped. "What do you want?"

"The groundhog saw his shadow," Mitchell declared. "That means six more weeks of winter." He paused to count the weeks from Groundhog Day on the wall calendar by the phone. "It's been more than seven weeks now."

"Thanks for the update, robo-brain," Haley groused. "Now I'm more depressed than ever."

"I think I have a cure for your seasonal affective disorder," her father, Perry, said. "What about a father-daughter weekend in our old stomping grounds?"

Haley was almost afraid to perk up at this appealing offer. What if it were some kind of trick? "By 'old stomping grounds,' you mean California, right?" she asked. "Are you serious?"

"Sure," Perry said. He'd been in a generous mood lately. Haley could only assume it was because his work was going well. "I've been invited to speak at a conference at UC-Berkeley next weekend: 'The Environmental Dialectic in Documentary Film.' You haven't been out West in a year or so—want to come with?"

Haley jumped up and threw her arms around her father's neck. "Definitely!" she cried.

"Good idea, Perry," Joan said. "It's been torture watching Haley mope around the house the last week or so."

"It hasn't exactly been a party here with you either," Haley said.

It wasn't like her to snap at her mother that way. Haley hadn't been feeling herself lately, though it was hard to say why. It had been a fairly eventful winter at school, full of scandals, breakups, eating disorders, humiliations, engagements, political intrigue. . . .

The Cocobot clique—Coco De Clerq, Sasha Lewis, Cecily Watson and Whitney Klein—had discovered that their male counterparts (Spencer Eton, Johnny Lane, Drew Napolitano and Reese Highland) had spent their winter break cavorting with swimsuit models. The girls broke up with the boys, disastrously, and now, except for Reese and Haley, were mostly back to-gether with them. Meanwhile, Whitney's mother and Sasha's father had announced their engagement, mak-ing Whit and Sasha soon-to-be-stepsisters. In other engagement news, nerdlinger Dave Metzger's mother planned to marry art teacher Rick Von, sending Dave screaming into the arms of girlfriend Annie Arm-strong and RoBro!, the robot brother he had created. Senior class brain Alex Martin had become a crucial cog in Governor Eleanor Eton's political machine, and art rebels Shaun Willkommen and Irene Chen tried to pry boy photographer Devon McKnight from the arms of irritating freshmeat Darcy Podowski.

What was Haley's place in all this chaos? She wasn't sure. After so much upheaval, the rest of the Hillsdale crowd seemed to be settling down again—but Haley felt a bit lost. Ever since spring break had ended, she'd been coming straight home from school, trying to make a dent in the mountain of homework threatening to overwhelm the last half of her junior year, and hanging with seven-year-old Mitchell in her free time—not the most exciting scenario. She could use a change of scene, and maybe a reminder of where she came from and who she used to be. Maybe a trip to San Fran was just what she needed.

"So, where are we staying?" she asked her father. "The Fairmont? The Orchard?"

"Hotel Durant," Perry said. "It's just off the Berkeley campus."

"We're not staying in the city?" Haley had been hoping for a trip to glamorous San Francisco, not sleepy, granola-flecked Berkeley. Besides, she was itching to see her old childhood best friend, Gretchen Waller, who lived in San Francisco. The last time Haley had seen her, Gretchen was auditioning for commercials and styling herself as a twenty-first-century Audrey Hepburn. Haley didn't think her mere presence could lure the new sleeker-than-thou Gretchen out to ho-hum Berkeley.

"I won't have much time for sightseeing," Perry said. "But there's plenty for you to do in Berkeley. . . ."

"What if I stayed at the Wallers' for the weekend?" Haley asked. "That way I could be with Gretchen while you're working."

Perry glanced at Joan. "I don't know—"

"It sounds fine to me," Joan said. "If it's okay with the Wallers. I'll give Judy a call tonight and see what she says."

"Dad?"

"I was hoping for some quality time with my daughter," Perry said. "But okay."

"Perfect!" Haley said. Things were starting to look brighter already, even if the sky was still gunmetal gray.

"Breakfast at Fisherman's Wharf, take one." Haley aimed her video camera at an outer wall of the famous San Francisco tourist attraction. "And . . . action! Go Gretchen!"

Gretchen strolled into the shot wearing her signature black sheath and oversized sunglasses, looking much like a black-haired Audrey Hepburn. She carried a huge bouquet of flowers in her arms. She paused at the wall, waiting for someone to walk by. It took only a minute before a very flamboyant drag queen strutted past. Gretchen gave her the flowers. The drag queen gave Gretchen a big hug and kiss, and then agreed to be interviewed.

"Are you kidding?" the drag queen said. "What kind of idiot would walk away from Audrey Hepburn?"

"What's your name?" Gretchen asked.

"Miss Taken," the drag queen replied.

"What's your favorite place in San Francisco?" Haley asked from behind the camera.

"The Candy Bar," Miss Taken said. "Of course. I sing there on Friday nights. You girls should stop by—especially if you like chocolate martinis."

"We would, only we're under twenty-one," Gretchen said.

"What? You're kidding me. You girls better get some beauty sleep—I thought you were at least twenty-five."

At Gretchen's slightly horrified look, Miss Taken added, "Just kidding, sweetheart. But seriously, sleep *is* the key to looking young. Remember that."

"I'll never forget it as long as I live," Gretchen said, the aspiring actress in her coming out full force.

"Good girl," Miss Taken said. "Well, I've got to run. See you girls around." Haley followed her with the camera until she turned a corner and walked out of sight.

"That was perfect!" Haley called, pausing the camera. "A very San Fran moment."

"Let's do it again," Gretchen said.

They interviewed a homeless man, an elegant older woman and a nanny leading two children by the hand. Gretchen was having the time of her life, and so was Haley. It had been a while since she'd used the video camera her dad had given her for Christmas a year earlier, and she'd forgotten how much she loved capturing people and places on film. She'd also forgotten how much fun hanging with Gretchen and her other old friends could be. The last time Haley had visited, things were a little awkward between her and her former bestie, but now that they were older, they were reestablishing their friendship on new footing.

Haley and Gretchen spent the rest of the day revisiting their favorite places, Haley shooting fascinating faces and architectural details she admired. They ended up meeting their old friend Harry and a few of Gretchen's new school friends at a sushi joint for dinner. Haley filmed the whole rowdy, laughing conversation.

"You seem different from last time you were

here," Gretchen said that night as they got ready for bed.

"In what way?" Haley asked. She felt different inside—a deep, inner calm—but she was surprised to hear it showed on the outside too.

"I don't know." Gretchen fluffed a down pillow and leaned back on it. Her jet-black hair made a nice contrast to the white pillowcase. Haley was tempted to take a quick shot of it with her camera, but decided she'd filmed Gretchen enough for one day. "You seem cooler, in a good way. Like, more sure of yourself somehow. More *yourself*. I think it's the camera."

"Really?" This surprised Haley. She'd expected Gretchen, actress and camera hog though she was, to get tired of being filmed after a while.

"Yeah. It's like, looking through the lens makes you see the world around you more, or something. Like it gives you courage somehow, to put yourself out there and take it all in."

"Wow, thanks." Haley was genuinely touched. She was enjoying the city more than ever now that she had her video camera in hand. It was as if it gave her a frame to see the world through, so that everything she saw became her own.

"Anyway, I'm sorry you have to leave tomorrow," Gretchen said. "You should come out more often."

"And you should come visit me in New Jersey," Haley said. "So you can see it's not just tacky malls, mullets and poufy hair."

"I don't think it's like that anymore," Gretchen said.

"Yes you do," Haley said. "I know you secretly do."

"Okay, I admit it. But if I come East we're spending time in Manhattan, not Paramus."

"Deal."

"We can do our 'girl on the street' interview show in New York, just like we did here," Gretchen said. "And maybe a casting agent will walk by and discover me!"

"Stranger things have happened," Haley said.

On the plane back to Newark, Haley showed her father the raw footage she'd shot in San Francisco. "Very impressive," Perry said. "Some of these scenes are beautifully framed. You have a real eye for this, Haley."

"I must take after my old man," Haley said, leaning against his shoulder.

When she got home, she threw herself into editing the footage, using her father's equipment. The lost feeling, that sense of not belonging, of being at sea, was suddenly gone. Her mother noticed the change in her, and even Mitchell sensed that something was different about his older sister. He tugged on her hair with his sticky fingers, hoping to get her attention. This time, instead of swatting him away, Haley turned to him and said calmly, "Yes?"

Mitchell looked stunned. Haley guessed that he didn't have anything to say. He just felt like touching her hair.

"Did you want something, Mitchie?" Haley said.

"You're different," Mitchell said.

"I see it too," Joan said. "You've grown up a bit over the weekend, Haley. It's almost like magic. What happened to that sulky little Snoodles who just last week whined about how bored she was?"

Haley shrugged. "I guess she found something to do."

"You should do something with that video footage," Perry said, watching over her shoulder as she edited. "It's too good to hide."

"Well, I need a spring art project for Mr. Von's class," Haley said. "I could use this for that. Or I could post it online, I guess."

"As a vlog," Perry said. "That would get you a wider audience, if you feel ready for it."

That was the question. Haley liked the footage she'd shot, but did she want everyone at school to see it—and judge it? She thought of Coco, who could cut her to shreds with one catty comment, and Devon, whose opinion as a fellow photographer carried a lot of weight with Haley. If they were going to see this video, it had to be just right—and that would take a lot more work.

On the other hand, if she saved the video for an art project, she'd have Mr. Von's help in shaping it before anyone else saw it. That route was safer, but not so independent.

● ● ●

At seventeen, Haley seems to have found her calling at last. As Gretchen pointed out, seeing the world through a camera lens helps Haley focus on her own personal vision. And that has brought Haley a lot of confidence.

The question now is: where should she take this new vision? Is she ready to throw herself onto the Internet, putting her artistic ego at the mercy of the mob? Or should she take her time and at least get Mr. Von's professional opinion first? It's up to you.

If you think Haley should use her video as an art project for Mr. Von's class, turn to page 18, ART PROJECT. If you think Haley should skip the academic opinion and post her footage online for all to see, turn to page 12, VIDEO DIARY.

This is a momentous time for Haley. Her junior year is drawing to a close. It's a last chance to make a lot of decisions that could permanently affect her future—and those decisions are all up to you.

Is it possible to be a sellout at seventeen?

Haley stayed in hermit mode for another week, spending hours in her room after school and on the weekend editing her San Francisco footage. When it was finally as good as she could make it, she uploaded the video and linked it to her profile on the Hillsdale High School Web site.

"I hope people will like it—if they even bother to watch it," she said to her father.

"It's brilliant," Perry said. "Not that I'm biased or anything. I think people will love it."

"Thanks, Dad." Haley felt nervous, sending such a personal work of art out into the world like this. Viewers would judge the film, comment on it or, worst of all, ignore it. She had a strangely protective feeling about it and just hoped it wouldn't get trashed.

"Kind of feels like sending your firstborn off to kindergarten, doesn't it?" Perry said.

Haley shrugged. "I wouldn't know about that."

"Trust me, it does," Perry said. "I still remember dropping you off at kindergarten the first day. I wanted to run inside and bring you back home, but I knew I couldn't do that. You've got to let go at some point. The best thing to do now is try to forget all about it."

Haley tried to take her father's advice, but it wasn't easy. About an hour after she first uploaded the film online, she gave in to temptation and checked her profile for comments.

"Haley, your video is amazing," Hannah Moss had written. "It makes me want to move to San Francisco right now!"

"Beautiful," Alex Martin had written. "I always knew you were an artiste at heart."

And from Coco De Clerq: "Everyone's raving about this video of yours. I guess it's all right, but what's with the fashion out there? I'm into boho chic as much as the next girl, but this video proves you can definitely overdo it."

Haley laughed off the comment. *You can't win 'em all,* she thought, and in this case Haley was flattered Coco had bothered to watch the video at all. Besides, Coco was *not* into boho chic. Gazillionaire chic was more her style. Or at the very least, high-status label-conscious chic.

Haley's cell phone rang, and the ID said "Whittles." Whitney Klein. Haley took the call.

"Haley, why didn't you tell me you were a genius?" Whitney said. "I've got Sasha on the line too, by the way."

"We saw your SF movie and were blown away," Sasha said.

"Blown out of our minds," Whitney added.

"Thanks," Haley said, her face getting hot. She was so glad she'd listened to her dad and not hidden her video after all her hard work. People were really responding to it.

"And it gave us a great idea," Sasha said. "We're in the middle of wedding-planning hell—"

"It's not hell," Whitney cut in. "It's fun. But it is taking up a lot of time."

"Time that could be spent doing more useful things, like writing songs or playing soccer," Sasha said.

"This is once in a lifetime, Sash," Whitney said. "It's worth putting a little energy into it."

Haley just sat back and listened while the two future stepsisters argued over how much they liked or didn't like planning their parents' upcoming wedding. Haley was amazed at how sisterly they'd become over the past year. When she had first met Whitney and Sasha, they were like oil and water: Sasha sporty and cool, Whitney Coco's insecure, fashion- and weight-obsessed sidekick. Their personalities hadn't changed so much, but each girl seemed to respect the other's differences a lot more.

"Anyway, Haley, the wedding is in a month and we've got nothing planned for the rehearsal dinner," Sasha said.

"We thought it would be so romantic to play a video at the dinner," Whitney said. "'Linda and Jonathan: The Story of Their Love.' Or something like that. And you would be the perfect person to make it! What do you think?"

Haley paused. Linda Klein and Jonathan Lewis's love story, as far as Haley knew, had a happy ending, but if she remembered right it had a kind of sordid beginning. Something about an affair, a scandalous divorce, a gambling problem and AA meetings. Haley assumed Whitney and Sasha didn't want her to put all that into the video, but who knew?

"Well, I've got a ton of schoolwork this spring . . . ," Haley began.

"Don't we all," Sasha said. "But this will be worth it—we'll pay you."

Wow, Haley thought. She'd made one video and already she was getting offers to do it for money. Still, was "The Story of Their Love" the kind of work she wanted to do as an artist? "How much freedom would I have?" she asked. "Could I do this any way I want?"

"Of course!" Whitney said. "Now that we've seen your work, we totally trust you."

"Just try not to make my dad look too skeevy," Sasha said.

"Oh, and my mom hates it when you shoot her from the back," Whitney said. "She thinks her butt is big. But other than that, go crazy."

Haley hesitated. Then the doorbell rang. She wasn't expecting anyone, but she hesitated a little longer just to wait and see who was at the door.

A moment later her mom yelled up the stairs, "Haley! Reese is here to see you!"

Haley nearly dropped the phone. It wasn't exactly strange that Reese Highland would stop by—after all, he lived right next door. But he was always so busy being Mr. Perfect Student-Athlete-Gentleman that he often didn't seem to have much time for fun, or for Haley.

"So Haley, what do you say?" Whitney said over the phone.

"I'll have to think about it," Haley said. "I'll call you back."

● ● ●

Haley has a chance to become a professional videographer— in a way. Somehow, being paid by your friends to make a tribute to their parents' love doesn't seem like the most

prestigious assignment you could get, but it's a start. And it might be fun, if the material is good.

But it took Haley a whole weekend of nonstop shooting just to get the San Francisco footage, and hours upon hours to shape it into something worth watching. Does she want to spend so much time on a video for Whitney and Sasha? Or does she have better things to do?

Speaking of better ways to spend time, there's a good example waiting for her at the door: the adorable Reese Highland. Haley might rather spend quality time with him instead of sitting alone in her room editing videotape on the subject of middle-aged love. She won't get paid for her time, but then, money isn't everything.

If you think Haley should agree to make the video for Sasha and Whitney, turn to page 33, LOVE STORY. If you think Haley ought to see what Reese wants before making a decision one way or the other, turn to page 26, HEART TO HEART.

Don't let fear of criticism hold you back—you could miss out on some heady praise.

"Haley, this is marvelous." Mr. Von rubbed his stubbly beard and gazed at the video monitor as Haley's images flashed by. "You've got a real eye for texture, which is hard to get across on video. Bravo."

Haley blushed. She'd decided to bring her finished San Francisco video to art class so that she could get feedback before she shared it with the public-at-large. Besides, she could use the class credit.

So she screened the short for Mr. Von and the art diehards taking advanced studio art with her, including Devon McKnight, Irene Chen and Shaun Willkommen. Devon sat at the back in his usual Mr. Cool uniform of jeans, an ironic T-shirt and leather jacket, his light brown hair hanging in his face. Irene wore a short Catholic-school kilt with over-the-knee boots and a thrift-store sweater, and had just gotten a haircut with supershort Cleopatra bangs. Shaun, with his blond crew cut, double chin and pudgy gut, was rocking an Evel Knievel–style jumpsuit.

"It really captures the feeling of the city," Irene said. "I feel like I'm there."

"I am so there," Shaun said. "Haley, it's like you took me to San Fran on a transporter beam. Doof esenihC rof yrgnuh em gnikam si kcilf siht."

Shaun had a gift: he could say any sentence backward without having to think about it. This gift had dubious usefulness, but it was part of what made Shaun Shaun. Haley was used to it by now, but Irene was still his most skillful translator.

"You're always hungry for Chinese food," Irene reminded him.

"Yeah, but now I can practically taste it," Shaun said. "Look at those salt-and-pepper crabs! Crunch!"

"What do you think, Dev?" Irene asked.

Haley held her breath as she waited for Devon's verdict. He was notoriously critical of most people's artwork, including his own. Haley couldn't help hoping he'd like her film. The two of them had bounced around between friendship and something

19

more, but Devon was hard to pin down. Haley knew that it wouldn't hurt things between them if her video impressed him.

"I think it's the work of a true auteur," Devon declared. "A Truffaut for our times."

Haley could breathe again.

"High praise indeed," Mr. Von said. "And I'd have to agree."

"Thanks." Haley's cheeks were burning. She loved the praise, but she blushed far too easily.

"Anyone else have a project to share today?" Mr. Von asked.

As Irene unveiled her latest collage, Haley spotted Darcy Podowski, a skinny, tattooed, platinum blond freshman, slipping into the classroom and into a seat next to Devon. Haley's nerves immediately jangled with irritation. Darcy lived near Devon in the Floods section of town, and used it as an excuse to tag along with him wherever he went. She always seemed to be around and in the way, Haley thought, but now she was infiltrating classes she wasn't even in? That was going too far.

Apparently, Devon thought so too. Darcy leaned close to whisper something to him, but before she had a chance to finish Devon got up and walked over to Mr. Von's desk. He picked up a hall pass and waved it at Mr. Von, who nodded. Mr. Von was notoriously liberal with hall passes. Devon headed for the boys' bathroom. Darcy waited a few minutes. *Brazen of her,* Haley thought. Finally Mr. Von said, "Ms. Podowski, I don't believe you belong in this class, do you? Can we help you with something?"

Darcy turned bright pink and muttered, "No, that's okay," and scuttled out of the room. A minute later Devon returned, almost as if he'd been waiting for her to leave.

"What was that all about?" Haley whispered to Irene.

"Beats me," Irene said. "I think Devon's dodging Darcy these days. About time."

Haley couldn't have agreed more. Haley, Devon, Irene and Shaun had made a cozy foursome until Darcy came along and made it an awkward five— with Haley usually the odd one out.

Shaun butted his head into their whispered conversation. "Bet you five bucks I know who you're talking about," he said with a wicked grin. "I have a proposal: everybody come over to my house after school today. That means you, Haley; you, Irene; me, Shaun; and him, Devon. That does not mean Darcy. I think Devon could use a little break from that chicklet, but she won't leave him alone, so I'm lending him Fort Willkommen to hide out in. You both in?"

"I'm in," Irene said.

"Me too," Haley said.

When class was over, Haley started to file out

after Shaun, Devon and Irene, but Mr. Von stopped her. "Stay a minute and talk," he said in his raspy voice.

Irene glanced back at Haley, who waved them on. "I'll be out in a minute," Haley said.

"I'm very impressed by your video work," Mr. Von said. "You've come a long way since last year. I see a lot more confidence in your artwork, a real sense of who you are. Nice job."

"Thanks," Haley said.

"I assume you know about the upcoming honors banquet," Mr. Von continued. Haley nodded. Every spring Hillsdale High held a banquet to hand out awards in all academic fields to outstanding juniors and seniors. Haley hadn't felt especially outstanding that year and wasn't expecting to go.

"It's my responsibility to choose the winner of the Lemmling Art Foundation Creativity Award," Mr. Von said. "I've been struggling with the decision all semester, but what I saw today made up my mind. Haley, I've chosen you to receive the Lemmling Award."

"Me?" Haley was stunned. Of all the academic or athletic prizes she might be up for, art was the one she had least expected to win. She was so glad she'd decided to save her video for art class! Knowing she was going to win an award for it flooded her with confidence and a determination to do more video work. "Thank you so much!"

"You're welcome," Mr. Von said. "It's well deserved.

I look forward to seeing you at the banquet next week, and please let your parents know that they're invited to attend as well."

"I will, thanks," Haley said. "They'll be thrilled."

"And very proud, I assume," Mr. Von said. "As they should be."

Haley couldn't wait to see her father's face when she told him the news. His daughter following in his footsteps was probably the last thing he ever expected. He'd be so proud he'd burst.

Just then Shaun popped his head into the room. "Hey, Haley, what's the holdup?" Mr. Von cast him a severe look. "Whoops. Sorry, Mr. V. I didn't realize you were having a heavy chat. Haley, we'll wait for you outside."

"It's all right, Haley," Mr. Von said. "You can go now. And congratulations."

Haley joined her friends in the hallway. "What was that all about?" Irene asked.

"It looked like you and Von were planning to take over the universe or something," Shaun said.

"No, nothing like that," Haley said. She suddenly felt shy about the good news Mr. Von had given her. Any one of her friends—Shaun, Irene, but especially Devon—would have loved to get the Lemmling Award. Any one of them would have deserved it, too. She decided not to tell them about it. If they ended up at the banquet and found out, fine. Otherwise, she'd tell only her parents.

"So are we hitting Shaun's today or what?" Devon said. "I'm telling you, I can't go home. Not until dark, at least. I've got to hide out."

Shaun threw a protective arm around Devon. "We've got your back, bro. No ninth grader is going to freak out one of our gang, right?"

"Right," Irene said. "Let's go."

Haley hesitated. She wanted to go to Shaun's house, but at the same time she was bursting with her news and couldn't wait to tell her parents.

● ● ●

Haley really seems to have found her niche with this video. Who knew she was such a budding auteur? If she were a brasher person, with an ego like, say, Coco De Clerq's, she'd be telling everyone in school the big news about the Lemmling Award. But Haley's sensitive, and her delicate feelers tell her that, while Devon might well be happy for her success, he also might be jealous. And hurt that he wasn't Mr. Von's chosen one. Haley doesn't want to hurt him or stir up any competition between her friends. While that may be admirable, it leaves her in a sticky spot. Will she be able to make it through a whole afternoon at Shaun's without blurting out the news? Or should she make her excuses and hurry home to tell her parents and plan her outfit for the banquet?

Meanwhile, what's up with Devon? His attitude toward Darcy suddenly seems to have changed a lot, but Haley doesn't know what's behind it. If she spends the afternoon with him, she might get a better picture of how he feels—about both Darcy and herself.

If you think Haley should see if Devon's interest in her is heating up, have her go with her arty friends to the Willkommens' manse on page 48, HIDE OUT AT SHAUN'S. If you think Haley should stop being so modest and put her freshly minted art career before Devon, go straight to the HONORS BANQUET on page 39.

A work of art can really
open people up.

"Hey, Reese." Haley had come downstairs to find Reese standing in the front foyer. His tan—from a winter holiday week in Aruba that Haley decided she'd rather not think about—had faded, but he didn't need a tan to look gorgeous. His tousled black hair and sea blue eyes still unnerved Haley, in the best way. "What's up?"

"I saw your movie online," Reese said. "I just wanted to tell you in person how much I liked it."

"Haley, why don't you invite Reese in for some

cocoa?" Haley's mother suggested. She meant unsweetened, dairy-free cocoa, Haley knew, which was hardly a treat.

"Oh, sorry." Haley had been so mesmerized by Reese's praise—he liked her movie!—that she'd forgotten her manners. "Come on into the kitchen."

Joan put the kettle on the stove and left Haley and Reese alone. "It looked so professional," Reese said. "Your video, I mean. How long were you in San Francisco?"

"Just a weekend," Haley said. "I stayed with an old friend and just filmed everything we did. We spent a lot of time stopping interesting-looking people on the street and doing impromptu interviews."

"That was one of my favorite parts!" Reese said. "The people you talked to on the street were so quirky."

Haley laughed. "One thing about San Francisco— it's not hard to find quirky people there."

"But they were more than that," Reese said. "They all had funny things to say, and a few of them were pretty profound. Like that truck driver who said he doesn't sweat it when he's stuck in traffic, because it makes him appreciate the flow of the city. That once the jam unsnarls, driving feels like a rush."

"That guy was a trip," Haley said. "He actually talked to us for half an hour, and I had to cut a lot of his better quips about the Zen of truck driving. I hated to do it, but I was afraid I'd lose the viewer's attention if I let him ramble on too long."

"The length of the film was perfect," Reese said. "It left me wanting more, actually. But the rhythm of the shots, the cuts between people talking and the beautiful buildings, and the sky, and the bay . . . it was just awesome."

Haley was nearly speechless. She couldn't remember ever hearing Reese praise her this enthusiastically for anything she'd done. She felt her cell phone buzzing in her pocket, but decided to ignore it to prolong this moment in the kitchen with Reese.

The kettle whistled. Haley got up and poured them each a cup of peppermint tea. "Trust me, you don't want this kind of cocoa." She showed him the package: "Virtuous Hot Chocolate."

Reese laughed. "Hot chocolate and virtue should not go together." He accepted a mug of tea. "I've been to San Francisco a few times, but I never saw the beauty of it the way you showed it in your work. I mean, obviously it's a pretty city and very cool to kick around in, but I never really *saw* it until I saw it through your eyes. It's like you showed me a new, magic city."

"Thank you, Reese," Haley said. "That has to be one of the best things anyone has ever said to me. I'll never forget it."

Her phone buzzed again. The vibration was beginning to distract and annoy her, so she pulled the phone out of her pocket. "I'd better take this before it buzzes a hole through my jeans," she said. She glanced at the screen; she'd missed nine calls from Whitney Klein, and this was the tenth one. She took it.

"Hey, Whit."

"Haley, why did you hang up so quickly?" Whitney said. "Listen, we know you're really busy—we all are, right? It's junior year! But it would mean so much to me and Sasha if you could make this video. Not just to us, but also to Mom and Jonathan. You'd be helping us give a really meaningful gift to our parents, a gift that will last a lifetime, that will help them get through the ups and downs of their new marriage. . . ."

While Whitney babbled on about the future of her mother's second marriage, Haley caught Reese watching her with a peculiar starry-eyed gaze. It was almost too intense, so she looked away and tried to focus on Whitney and Sasha's pleas for Haley to turn their parents' romance into a work of art. But with Reese there goggling at her, she couldn't concentrate.

"Whitney, let me call you back," she said into the phone. "I promise I'll think about it very hard." She clicked off.

"Another fan calling to tell you what a genius you are?" Reese said.

"Not really," Haley said. "Just Whitney and Sasha freaking out over their parents' wedding."

"There's something different about you lately, Haley," Reese said. "You seem more confident than you did last winter. I remember thinking you were confident when we first met, but then it seemed like the Hillsdale craziness kind of got to you."

"It can be pretty crazy."

"But in the middle of all that craziness you seem totally sane," Reese said. "It's almost like you're the only sane person in the whole school."

Haley shuddered slightly. She had to admit that there'd been a time when hearing adoring words like this from Reese would have thrilled her to tears. But at that moment, she found it overwhelming and a little creepy.

"Well, I wouldn't go that far," Haley said. "What about you? You seem pretty together."

"I know I can look that way from the outside," Reese said. "But inside is another story."

Haley wasn't sure whether to believe him or not. It wasn't unusual for boys to claim to be all torn up inside but unable to show their emotions. In Reese's case, however, he really had seemed pretty centered— until now. Haley didn't quite know how to handle it. Maybe the best thing to do was just to change the subject.

"How's the track team looking this spring?" she said. "I heard Cecily Watson is running the fifty-meter sprint in record time."

Reese didn't answer. Instead he leaned toward her, closed his eyes and puckered up.

"Whoa." Haley involuntarily jumped back.

Reese's eyes sprang open and he blinked. Not too many girls had turned down a kiss from Reese Highland before, Haley was sure of that.

"I'm sorry," he said. "Was that out of line? It's just that, ever since I saw that video you made, I've felt such a connection with you. . . ."

Haley was flattered, but it didn't make her want to kiss him more. "You weren't out of line," she said. "It's just . . . I'm not sure I'm ready to get back together. I mean, before we know it we'll be leaving for college—"

"College is still a year away," Reese reminded her.

"I know, but both of us are so busy, you know that time is going to fly by," Haley said. "I just don't see how we would have time for each other . . . and with our history, I don't feel we could just casually date, you know? We're both pretty intense people."

Reese didn't put up any protest, though Haley could see that she'd upset him. She wasn't sure why she had said what she did; it had just poured out of her. Maybe Reese and her mother were right; maybe she really had changed. It was the only explanation.

"All I'm saying is," she heard herself say, "we're too young to be serious. Don't you think?"

Reese smiled ruefully and shook his head. "I guess that makes sense. If that's the way you feel, I'll respect that." He got up to go. "Well, see you in AP History tomorrow."

"Thanks," she said, while her brain was screaming,

What did you just do? You turned down Reese Highland? Are you crazy?

Meanwhile, her cell buzzed once again. She didn't need to glance at it to know who was calling: Whitney and Sasha. Again.

● ● ●

Lucky Haley—she's swamped with options, but is it more than she can handle? Junior year is always a busy time, especially the second semester, and Haley can't do everything. Clearly she's decided to set aside Reese's sudden advances in favor of being more sensible and productive. But which part of her life should she focus on? There's her academic life, her new artistic-professional life and her social life—the prom. She may be swearing off boys for the time being, but that doesn't mean she doesn't want to go. After all, the prom is more than just an ordinary dance. It's a milestone.

If you think Haley should focus on her schoolwork, send her back to class on page 55, MAKING HISTORY. If you think Haley should advance her filmmaking chops by creating a pre-wedding video for the Klein-Lewis rehearsal dinner, go to page 61, PERFECT MATCH. Finally, if you think Haley's ready to start thinking about the prom, which is right around the corner, go to page 71, FOUR DRESSES.

A picture's worth a thousand words, but then, anything's better than bad poetry.

"We want it supercandid," Whitney said. "That's why you're so perfect for the job—because Jon and Mom are so used to seeing you around. If we hired some stranger to follow after them filming their every move, they'd notice, obviously."

"But that's not the only reason we want you," Sasha added. "It's mostly because we think you're brilliant."

Haley nodded skeptically. They'd met at Bean Town, a local coffee shop, to talk over Whitney and

Sasha's proposal that Haley film the pre-wedding preparations of Whitney's mother, Linda Klein, and Sasha's father, Jonathan Lewis. The girls were looking forward to becoming official stepsisters and wanted to show their parents how excited they were.

Haley was still having trouble getting used to the idea of Sasha Lewis and Whitney Klein as sisters. Both girls were blond, but the resemblance ended there. Sasha was tall and cool with long legs and long straight hair. She was a soccer star and a great singer-songwriter who'd played by herself and in a band with her boyfriend, Johnny Lane. She was a multi-talented golden girl with a good heart and a lot of confidence.

Whitney, on the other hand, was bubbly and curvy, and mainly interested in fashion and gossip. She was a recovering shoplifter and binge-eater who now had a thriving business designing her own clothes. She could be a little spacey, but, like Sasha, she was a nice person—and that was the important part, Haley thought.

"How exactly do you want to do this?" Haley asked.

"Mom and Jon's love is really special," Whitney said. "Before we came up with the movie idea, I thought I could read a poem at the rehearsal dinner. Want to hear it?"

"Go for it," Haley said.

Whitney pulled a notebook from her bag, opened it, cleared her throat and began to read.

> "Ode to Linda and Jon:
> When my dad left my mom
> For that skank named Trish
> My mom's heart was bloody and sore.
> I know, 'cause I heard her crying every
> night
> Through the door.
>
> She drank too much and went to AA
> Where she met Jonathan Lewis,
> A gamblin' man who gambled so much
> He nearly blew it.
> Jon saved Linda, and Linda saved Jon
> Without him her sanity would probably
> be gone.
>
> But now they're so happy,
> Now they're ecstatic,
> The question of marriage was quite
> automatic—"

"I think that's enough," Haley said, cringing. Poetry was definitely not Whitney's forte. "I get the picture."

"I still might want to read it at the rehearsal

dinner," Whitney said. "I mean, we can have a movie and a poem too."

"No, Whitney—remember, we agreed," Sasha said diplomatically. "Their love is impossible to put into words."

"Sasha's right," Haley said. "There's no way to put this—this level of emotion into words." She was trying to spare Whitney the embarrassment—and everyone else the pain—of what had to be the worst poem ever written.

"We want you to be there for their wedding preparations," Whitney said. "Follow them around with your video camera. It would be great if you could hide the camera somehow, but if you can't, just say you're making a video about the American teen or something. Mom would buy that."

"My dad would totally think we were just taping each other," Sasha said.

"Show all the little things they do for each other as they get ready to pledge their hearts and souls in marriage," Whitney said. "All the things they do that say 'I love you.'"

"That sounds like it's going to take up a lot of time," Haley said. "I've got tons of other things to do—"

"It'll only take a week or so," Sasha said. "And we'll pay you! To make it worth your while."

Haley considered this. Making a video testament to Linda and Jonathan's love didn't strike her as the most creative use of her talents. If she wanted her next film project to be as arty and innovative as her last one, this wouldn't be the one she'd choose.

But if she looked at this project as an after-school job, it didn't seem so bad. It would be good to have a professional video gig to her credit already, at seventeen, and it would beef up her college applications. And she could definitely use the cash. The prom was coming up, and no matter who she ended up going with, she wanted to get a killer dress. Killer dresses cost money. Unless her mother offered to pony up for one, which Haley couldn't count on. Joan Miller's usual Green Earth sermon often included strong anti-consumerist ranting on such topics as why would a teenaged girl like Haley need so many new clothes. So unless Joan was feeling sentimental—not unheard of—Haley would have to get her own dress.

"Come on, Haley—please," Whitney wheedled. "It will be totally fun—just like hanging with your girlfriends, only with a video camera running."

"What do you say?" Sasha asked.

● ● ●

Haley has to decide if portraying the love story of two people she barely knows is worth the time she'll have to spend on it. Is this project beneath her creative talents? Or is any experience good experience? And then there's the money, which will go a long way toward funding the perfect prom dress.

But if she spends all her time making a pre-wedding video, will she have time for anything else—like schoolwork, or getting a date for the prom? What good is a killer dress if you don't have the killer date to go with it?

If you think Haley should do the video, go to page 61, PERFECT MATCH. If you think the video's a waste of time and she should start planning for the prom pronto, go to page 71, FOUR DRESSES.

HONORS BANQUET

Nothing levels the playing field like a roomful of beaming parents.

"This is one of the happiest days of my life, Snoodles," Perry Miller said, kissing the top of Haley's head.

"We really are very proud of you, Haley," Joan Miller added.

Haley tried to stifle the embarrassment her parents' praise often made her feel. After all, she had earned this. She'd worked hard on her video, and she could feel, deep inside, that making the film had somehow jump-started a powerful creative force within her that was only beginning to blossom.

"You're at table six," the girl at the door said, checking the Millers off her guest list. The school auditorium had been turned into a banquet hall, complete with round tables, tablecloths, centerpieces and freshman and sophomore "cater-waiters." The food was, unfortunately, gussied-up cafeteria fare—Haley could tell by the smell—but she appreciated the effort the school had made to make the banquet feel special.

As she threaded her way through the tables to her place, trailed by her parents, Haley searched the room for familiar faces. Out of modesty, she hadn't told anyone that Mr. Von had chosen her to receive the Lemmling Art Foundation Creativity Award, because she had no idea who else had won something, and only award winners and their guests were invited to the banquet. She didn't want to make anyone feel left out, least of all Irene, Shaun or Devon, none of whom was there.

She did spot Hannah Moss, tiny genius, with her physicist parents in tow. Hannah's parents were almost as small as she was. Haley was sure Hannah had won some kind of math or science prize. At the table next to Hannah's sat Dave Metzger and his girlfriend, Annie Armstrong. Haley's mother spotted them too and waved to Annie's mother, Blythe, who worked at the same law firm as Joan. Next to Blythe sat Annie's father, Doug, who Haley always thought was almost freakishly similar in looks and manner to Dave. And on the other side of Dave were his mother, Nora, and her fiancé, Mr. Von. Poor Dave was always a sensitive, nervous sort, with his multiple food allergies and his father out of the picture, but the engagement of Nora and Mr. Von seemed to have sent Dave over the edge. Haley couldn't help noticing that he was having a bit of an acne flare-up. His mother was sitting between him and Annie, which surprised Haley. Usually Dave and Annie liked to hold hands whenever possible.

"Oh, look, there are the Highlands," Haley's mother said, pointing at Reese's family two tables away. "Let's go say hello."

Haley set her bag at her place and followed her parents to the Highlands' table. She wasn't surprised to see Reese at the banquet—it was just like him to be honored for some aspect of his greatness. The only question was, which one.

"Hey there, neighbors," Oliver Highland greeted them. "Fancy meeting you here."

"Reese is getting the Terence McCafferty Memorial History Award," Barbara Highland said. "For the most talented junior historian."

"Okay, Mom, they'll find out soon enough," Reese said. Haley was a little touched to see how awkward Mr. Perfect could be when his parents were around.

"This is certainly a very happy occasion," Joan Miller said.

"What honor is Haley getting?" Oliver asked.

"The Lemmling Art Foundation Creativity Award," Perry said proudly.

"Oh, that's my favorite prize," Barbara Highland said. "I used to work for the Lemmling Foundation. Congratulations, Haley. I had no idea you were so creative!"

"She made this video in San Francisco that's really beautiful," Reese said.

"It's really not that big a deal," Haley said.

Perry threw his arm around her. "Now, don't be so modest. My daughter is brilliant! There, I said it."

"Dad—"

"We'd better sit down before our pride gets out of hand," Joan said. "Congratulations, Reese."

As they moved toward their table, Haley spotted Alex Martin coming into the room with his parents, Mary and Peter. Alex, a supersmart senior, looked snappy in his blue blazer and khaki pants, his short chestnut hair neatly combed and parted on the side. Haley wondered what award he'd won. He was a champion debater and very into politics—he'd worked for the new Republican governor of New Jersey, Eleanor Eton—so it was probably something in that realm. She also couldn't help thinking that he was totally cute in his conservative way, and only getting cuter with time. Too bad he was graduating so soon, and then going off to Georgetown for college. Haley wondered how often an ambitious guy like him would be seen around a small town like Hillsdale once he'd left.

Alex gave Haley a friendly nod as he and his family settled at the table next to the Millers'. Principal Crum took the stage to start the proceedings.

"Good evening, Hillsdale parents and students," Principal Crum said into a squeaky microphone. "This is always one of my favorite events of the year. For one thing, the only students allowed in are the good ones."

He paused for a laugh, but none came. Apparently he felt the need to explain his joke—always a big mistake—because he added, "I mean, the more delinquent students usually aren't up for academic awards, so we never have any problems at these banquets."

Perry Miller leaned close to Haley and whispered in her ear, "This guy's a real windbag, isn't he?"

Haley nodded and stifled a giggle. Though if she'd laughed out loud, Principal Crum would probably have been pleased.

Principal Crum cleared his throat. "In any case, I'm glad you're all here, and I'll be your master of ceremonies tonight. While the waiters take your drink orders and pass out the salads, let's bring up Cosmo Milosevic, our calculus teacher, to give out the first awards of the evening in the math and science categories."

Mr. Milosevic, a thin, lanky man in baggy pants

and owlish glasses, shambled up to the podium. "Thank you, Principal Crum. Without further ado, I'd like to give out the Melvin Heimlich Award for outstanding work in the field of physics. This year's prize goes to one of the most talented young physicists I've ever come across, Hannah Moss."

The room burst into applause as Hannah mounted the stage to accept a plaque from Mr. Milosevic. Dave Metzger yelled, "Go, Hannah!" and raised his fist triumphantly in the air. Hannah shook her math teacher's hand and went back to her table to kiss both her parents on the cheek.

"And now for the Dieter Kornbluth Prize in calculus," Mr. Milosevic went on. Haley tuned him out, distracted by what looked to her like an odd coldness between Dave and Annie. Dave seemed thrilled for Hannah, but Annie's congratulations seemed more polite than heartfelt. Haley knew that Dave and Annie had spent spring break together—had something happened to cause tension between them? Annie actually looked angry and avoided Dave's eyes.

Maybe it's Hannah, Haley thought. Dave and Hannah had a supertight friendship based on their shared scientific brilliance. Annie was more of a word person than they were, a good debater and writer rather than scientist, and she might have felt left out or even jealous—especially since Dave and Hannah had built RoBro!, Dave's robot brother, together. RoBro! had come to mean a lot to Dave, and he was constantly calling Hannah to come over and tinker with him.

Or maybe the problem is RoBro! himself, Haley thought. Perhaps the geek lovers had gotten their wires crossed over how much time Dave spent with the robot and how emotional he was over what Annie must have considered a screwed-together pile of metal. Annie had been supportive of RoBro! at first, because she knew Dave had been rejected by his father and was upset about it. But after a while it seemed as if RoBro! meant more to Dave than anyone—even Annie. Maybe Annie had reached her boiling point over that little issue.

"And last but certainly not least," Mr. Milosevic was saying when Haley turned her attention back to the stage, "I'm proud to present the Young American Scientific Achievement of Excellence Award to . . . David Metzger."

Dave's mother, Mr. Von and Hannah applauded and cheered as Dave made his way up to the stage. Annie clapped politely. Dave accepted his plaque, shook Mr. Milosevic's hand, waved nerdily to the crowd and stumbled over his big feet on the way back to his table. Nora Metzger stood up and hugged him, Mr. Von shook his hand and Hannah jumped up and down clapping. Annie, on the other hand, barely managed a "Congratulations" before turning her attention to her salad plate.

Very strange, Haley thought.

She didn't have a lot of time to think about it, because Mr. Von took the stage next to announce the artistic awards. He gave out the Mary Parker Prize for best student painting by a senior, and the Joseph Damon Award for improvement in ceramics. "And now, the winner of the Lemmling Art Foundation Creativity Award," he said.

Haley's spine tensed slightly. Her mother squeezed her hand.

"This award goes to the student who shows the most originality and discipline in a creative work of visual art of any format, whether painting, sculpture, photography, film, video or some new form that hasn't been invented yet."

The audience laughed lightly. Haley was in a daze as she listened to Mr. Von's description of the award. She could hardly believe he was talking about something *she'd* made, about *her*. It was thrilling.

"This year I'm pleased to present the award to a young woman who made a video that showcases the strange beauty of an American city and its people. The Lemmling Art Foundation Creativity Award goes to Haley Miller."

In a happy fog of cheering and applause, Haley made her way up to the stage. Mr. Von shook her hand and gave her a plaque. She blinked and smiled, hardly knowing what she was doing. Then she returned to her table. Her mother squeezed her tight and kissed her. Her father hugged her and said, "We are so proud of you."

Haley sat down and caught her breath. At the next table, Alex Martin grinned and gave her a joyous thumbs-up. Two tables away on the left, Reese Highland whooped and hollered for her.

It was a very good feeling.

● ● ●

Haley's on a roll. She's on fire at school, winning a prestigious award and impressing everyone with her video chops. And she's got two very hot boys—at *least* two—expressing major romantic interest in her. Either Alex or Reese would make a fine prom date, but they're not the only possibilities. Now that she's an award-winning artist, Haley might prefer to date one of her own kind—a fellow artist like Devon. Or perhaps fate has a prom-date surprise in store for her.

If you think Haley should try to continue her hot streak by focusing on high achievement at school—after all, it seems to be working for her—go to page 55, MAKING HISTORY. If you think Haley's ready to start thinking about the prom, turn to page 71, FOUR DRESSES.

HIDE OUT AT SHAUN'S

Come out, come out, wherever you are . . .

"It's driving me crazy," Devon said. "She shows up on my doorstep before school, asking for a ride. After school, she's waiting for me on the hood of the car like some kind of auto-show model. If I manage to sneak out of school before she catches me, she shows up on my doorstep again, expecting to spend the whole afternoon with me."

Shaun shook his head sympathetically. "That's rough, bro."

Irene punched him in the arm. "Oh, yeah, like you wouldn't eat that up."

Haley had come back to Shaun's house after school with Devon and Irene. They'd hidden Devon in Shaun's car so that he could slip away undetected by Darcy, who was driving Devon crazy.

"Don't worry, Devo, there's no way Darcy will find you here at Fort Willkommen," Shaun assured him. Haley looked around at the floor-to-ceiling glass windows all over the Willkommens' luxurious modern house and wondered how true that was.

"Please," Irene said. "All she has to do is press her little turned-up nose against that window and she can pick you out like a puppy in a pound."

"It's getting kind of scary," Devon said. "Darcy's obsessed with me. She won't leave me alone for a minute. If I'm not home, she hangs around my house and waits for me and starts pestering Shana. Shana used to like her but I think even she's getting weirded out by Darcy."

Shana was Devon's little sister, an adorable girl about Mitchell's age. Haley knew that Devon was very protective of her. The fastest road to alienating Devon was to threaten Shana in some way. Haley suddenly realized she felt protective of Mitchell, too, and she hadn't been spending enough time with him lately.

"That is creepy," she said to Devon. "To be using your little sister to get to you."

"Exactly," Devon said. "Darcy's all fake-sweet with Shana because she thinks I'll like that. It makes me sick."

Haley was intrigued by this shift in Devon's attitude toward Darcy. Only a few months earlier he'd seemed heavily into his freshman neighbor. Now she made him sick? Quite a big change. Haley wondered what was really behind it. Had Darcy simply worn out her welcome, or had something big gone down between the two of them? In any case, Haley was glad to jettison that fifth wheel and have the original foursome back together again. Without Darcy around, Devon was a lot friendlier and chattier.

"I don't know what to do," Devon went on. "I can't hide out here every day."

"Why not?" Shaun tossed a green olive in the air and caught it in his mouth. "We've got everything you need: a guest room, cable TV, video games and all the cheese doodles and banana ice cream you can eat. As well as a lot of other food."

"Yeah, if you like weird food combinations like olives and tapioca pudding, or anchovies with sour cream potato chips, this is your mecca," Irene said.

"That's no weirder than thousand-year-old eggs," Shaun said.

"We don't serve thousand-year-old eggs," Irene said. Her parents owned Golden Dynasty, a local Chinese restaurant. "And anyway, thousand-year-old eggs are an ancient delicacy, and anchovy-sour-cream potato chips are a junk food snack you just made up last week."

"Busted," Shaun admitted with a grin.

"I bet your aunt Mimi serves thousand-year-old eggs at her place in Frisco," Devon said to Irene.

"Oohhhh," Shaun said, drooling. "Remember the soup dumplings we had there? Now that's an authentic Chinese restaurant."

Irene punched Shaun in the arm. "Like you'd know."

"Ow." Shaun rubbed his bicep. "Stop giving me a Hertz donut."

The first time Haley had visited her old friend Gretchen, a year before, Shaun, Irene and Devon had met her there for a few San Francisco adventures. That was before Haley even knew Darcy Podowski existed.

"Your flick really blew me away, Haley," Devon said, "speaking of Frisco. It's the coolest short film I've seen in a while. I went to the New York Underground Film Festival a couple of weeks ago and nothing I saw there was nearly as good."

"Wow. Thanks, Devon," Haley said.

"You should think about entering it in a film festival," Devon said. "I'm serious."

"Maybe I will," Haley said. She hadn't thought of going the festival route, but it might be fun. People could see her video all over the world, from Berlin to Venice to Toronto. . . .

Devon settled on a stool behind the kitchen counter and helped himself to some cashews. "I always knew you were smart," he said. "But after I saw your film I realized there's more to you than that." He paused as if searching for the right word. "It's like, you've got soul."

"You got soul, girl!" Shaun shouted. "Hallelujah! Oh, wait." Shaun froze like a deer in headlights. "I think I heard something. Did you hear something?"

Everyone stayed perfectly still, listening. Haley thought she could hear something moving outside on the back patio.

"I think I hear something tapping on the window," Irene whispered.

"What if it's Darcy?" Shaun whispered back. "Everybody duck!"

They all crouched down behind the kitchen counter. "How can we see who's out there if we're all hiding down here?" Haley asked.

"Shhh!" Shaun put his finger to his lips. "We don't want Fatal Attraction to find us!"

"Darcy's really not *that* bad," Devon said. "I mean, not *Fatal Attraction* bad. She wouldn't kill someone's pet rabbit—I don't think. . . ."

Devon leaned against a cabinet and suddenly noticed the bowl of cashews in his hand. He passed it to Haley. "Nuts?"

She giggled and took a handful. "I'm not nuts. How about you?"

"I'm not nuts, either," Devon joked. "I'm a legume."

Haley laughed harder. "That doesn't even make sense."

"You guys, be quiet!" Shaun said. "You're laughing now, but it won't be so funny when Darcy busts in here with a bloody butcher knife."

That made Irene start laughing, which made Haley and Devon laugh even harder. Haley couldn't be sure if Shaun's straight face was serious or a put-on.

"Well, it's obvious none of you have seen *Friday the Thirteenth Part Eleventy-hundred,* because if you did you'd know we're in deep doo-doo here."

"Come on, Shaun, there's nobody out there." Haley bravely rose to her feet and peeked through the glass door. "It's raining," she announced. "That's what we heard—raindrops."

"Seriously?" Shaun cautiously poked his head over the counter. "There's no knife-wielding crazy girl out there?"

"No, but there's one right here!" Irene leaped up and tackled Shaun, who tumbled to the floor, finally laughing. She tickled him and wrestled him until she had him pinned to the Italian tile.

"Help! Tickling is a form of abuse!" Shaun cried through his helpless giggles.

"False alarm," Devon said, standing up and going to the fridge for a soda. "I should chill a bit. I'm way too tense. Sorry, guys."

"It was Shaun's fault," Irene said. "Him and his imagination."

Devon poured a glass of soda and handed it to Haley. She took it and he clinked glasses with her.

"It's nice to have things back to normal again, isn't it?" he said in a kind of toast.

Flattered, Haley thought, *It definitely is.*

● ● ●

As Devon said, things seem to be back to normal—well, as normal as they can ever be with Shaun around—with the cool art clique. And with Darcy not only out of the picture but Public Enemy Number One, Haley's in a great spot to scoop Devon up for herself. He's certainly sending signals that he's ripe for the picking. And Haley must be tempted. But before she makes a move, she must decide if Devon is what she really wants. If he asks her to the prom, what would she say? She'd better make up her mind before things go much farther. She could turn him off permanently if he thinks she's jerking him around.

Another boy is calling out to Haley from the back of her mind, demanding attention, and that boy is her little brother, Mitchell. Hearing Devon's protective talk about Shana has made Haley realize she hasn't been the sister to Mitchell that she could be. He's always been a bit troubled, a little different to say the least, and could use some love from his big sister.

If you think Haley should address her sisterly duty, have her take Mitchell to the PLAYGROUND on page 76. If you think she's too wound-up to give him any real attention and wants to look ahead to prom night, go to page 71, FOUR DRESSES.

MAKING HISTORY

Those who don't study for AP History are doomed to repeat it.

"**N**ame one of the treaties that ended World War One," Travis Tygert, Haley's AP History teacher, asked. Haley raised her hand. "Haley?"

"The Treaty of Versailles," Haley answered. "June twenty-eighth, 1919."

"Very good." Mr. Tygert swept his sandy hair off his golden-brown face and tapped France on the huge wall map of the world circa 1914. "The Allied governments forced the defeated Germans to give up much of the territory they'd taken and pay reparations to the

Allies, among other concessions." Boyish Mr. Tygert was gorgeous, the hottest teacher at Hillsdale by far, in most girls' opinions, as well as the coach of the girls' soccer team. When Haley had first arrived at Hillsdale she suffered a monster crush on him, but that had mercifully passed. Still, during slow periods in class she found herself admiring the cinnamon sprinkle of freckles on his nose and forearms with a dreamy sigh.

This was no time for daydreaming, though. Haley was determined to score well on her AP History exam, so she'd been studying hard and catching up on her reading. It was now paying off.

"Can anyone name another important World War One treaty?" Mr. Tygert asked.

Haley and Reese both raised their hands. Mr. Tygert called on Reese.

"The Treaty of St. Germain," Reese replied.

"Correct. Date?"

Reese hesitated. Haley raised her hand.

"September tenth, 1919. St. Germain was the Allies' peace treaty with the Austro-Hungarian Empire. It basically broke up the empire into a lot of small, independent states."

"Great answer, Haley," Mr. Tygert said. "You're on fire today."

Reese nodded at her, impressed. Haley smiled. She felt invincible, as if she could answer any question Mr. Tygert threw her way.

"Let's talk about the years leading up to World War Two," Mr. Tygert said. "Alex, would you change the map, please?"

Alex Martin, the senior and ace history student, worked as Mr. Tygert's teaching assistant for Haley's AP History class. He usually sat at the front of the room grading quizzes or listening to the discussion. He stood up and pulled a world map from 1919 over the one from 1914. The outlines of many countries in Europe suddenly changed.

"As you should have read in your textbooks, Adolf Hitler was a German soldier in World War One. Who can tell me how his experience contributed to the rise of fascism in Germany and the events of World War Two?"

Haley raised her hand again. "The German defeat was demoralizing and made a lot of Germans angry, including Hitler. He believed that the Germans could have won the war if they hadn't given up too soon. And he blamed Allied propaganda for convincing the Germans that they couldn't win."

She glanced over at Reese, who looked more impressed than ever. Even Alex, in his spot next to Mr. Tygert's desk, looked surprised at the complexity of her answer.

"Very good," Mr. Tygert said. "So he decided he would use propaganda himself—and use it better than the Allies ever did. Hitler's rousing speeches and slogans, combined with desperate poverty and anger in Germany, brought about a mob mentality that led to the rise of the Nazi Party. Haley, I have a feeling you're going to do great on your AP exam."

Haley blushed.

"Alex, would you pass back yesterday's quizzes?" Mr. Tygert said, taking a seat at his desk. Alex passed the graded quizzes around the room. He stopped at Haley's desk and handed her a paper marked *99—A*.

"You got the highest score in the class," he whispered. "I don't think I'm supposed to tell you that, but just this once . . ."

The bell rang and class was over. Haley gathered her books and got up to leave. Reese stopped her at the door.

"You're really on top of your twentieth-century history," he said.

Haley shrugged coolly, as if it were no big deal. "It's just a matter of doing the reading—"

"—and understanding it and retaining it," Reese said.

Alex paused next to them on his way out of class. "Nice work today, Miller. You really know your stuff."

"Thanks."

"I was thinking—" Alex began, but before he could finish his sentence Reese cut in.

"Do you want to come over to my house later to study?"

Alex said almost the exact same words at the exact same time. He and Reese glared at each other.

Boys, Haley thought. *They're so competitive.*

"We can help each other prep for the test," Reese said.

"I already took the test," Alex countered. "And I got the highest score possible. I can help you do the same."

"That's cheating," Reese said.

"Tutoring isn't cheating," Alex said. "Besides, you can help me study too, Haley, and get a head start on next year's history."

Haley glanced from one to the other, unsure what to do. She didn't want to offend either one of them, and she wasn't sure she wanted to spend that afternoon studying history anyway.

"Come on, Haley," Reese said in a coaxing voice, with that adorable twinkle in his blue eyes. "I'm right next door. If you need a study break, we can go outside and shoot hoops."

"I've got a new laptop you can use," Alex said. "And my parents won't be home until late."

Haley sighed. "Hmm," she said. "I've done pretty well studying by myself. But I guess I should pick a study buddy. . . ."

●　●　●

Haley's brainy coolness is driving the smart boys wild. She showed in class that she doesn't need them—they

need her. But having a study buddy couldn't hurt, and each boy has his advantages. . . .

Haley has always been intrigued by Alex. He's a little older, obviously very smart and successful at everything he tries. His cute preppy looks don't hurt, either. Haley is flattered by his attention, and it reflects well on her. There's chemistry between them too. But Alex is graduating soon and leaving for college in the fall. What will happen then? If she gets too close to him, isn't there a good chance she'll get hurt?

Reese is conveniently next door, but Haley hasn't always been able to keep his attention. He clearly likes high achievers, and now that Haley's working at the top level, he's gaga over her. This could be Haley's best chance to spend a lot of quality time with him and seal her place in his heart.

If you think Haley should learn from a master, have her STUDY WITH ALEX on page 91. If you think Haley's heart belongs to Reese, no matter how much she may try to deny it, go to page 84, STUDY WITH REESE.

Her academic future—and more—depends on your choice.

PERFECT MATCH

There's a fine line between sweet and icky.

"First stop, L'Armoire," Coco said as she steered her convertible through the streets of Hillsdale. "Is it too chilly to put the top down?"

Haley glanced through the windshield at the gray day and shivered. "Yes, it's too chilly."

Coco sighed. "I can't wait for real spring to start. It always seems to take forever."

Haley rode with her in the front seat as they followed Sasha and her father, Jonathan, to the upscale shop at the mall. Sasha was helping Jonathan with his pre-wedding errands by chauffeuring him in her beloved red 1969 Mustang Stallion. The plan was to have Coco and Haley "accidentally" bump into them so that Haley could secretly film Jonathan as he prepped for the big celebration. Then, if they could pull it off, Coco and Haley would tag along for the rest of the day, surreptitiously taping everything he did. Later on, Coco and Haley would "accidentally" meet up with Whitney and her mother to do the same secret videotaping.

Haley had her video camera concealed in her bag. "I don't see how her father won't notice," she said. "I mean, my camera is small but not that small."

"Trust me, he's so blissed out in love he doesn't notice anything," Coco said, her sweet words tempered by a slightly disgusted tone. "Except his fiancée's gorgeous eyes."

"Aww," Haley said. "Coco, I had no idea you were such a sucker for love."

Coco wrinkled her finely shaped nose until her large designer sunglasses nearly fell off. "Coco De Clerq is no one's sucker. You should know that by now, Haley."

"Oh, I do, I do. Thanks for coming with me today, by the way."

"I like to think of myself as a patroness of the arts," Coco said.

This was the first day of Haley's after-school job making a pre-wedding video for Whitney and

Sasha's parents. Haley wondered why Coco had volunteered to keep her company—she claimed it was because she had admired Haley's video work so much. That didn't sound like the usual Coco motivation, but Haley had nothing else to go on.

"You seem to be in a good mood," Haley said, fishing for information. Coco took the bait.

"Oh, I am," Coco said. "Haven't you heard the news? Mia Delgado is not coming back to Hillsdale!"

"She's not?" Haley had somehow missed this juicy piece of gossip. Mia Delgado was an exchange student from Madrid who also happened to be a fashion model, statuesque and gorgeous with masses of long black hair. "Why not?"

"She landed some kind of big-deal modeling contract in Paris," Coco said.

"Wow. Good for her."

"Yeah," Coco said. "Good for her, even better for us. Who needs that kind of competition around? I mean, *I* never thought she was so hot, but a lot of the boys couldn't keep their tongues in their mouths when she was around. It was gross. Good riddance."

"What about Sebastian?" Haley asked. Sebastian Bodega was also a gorgeous Spanish exchange student and off-and-on boyfriend of Mia's. "I haven't seen him since before Christmas."

"He's not coming back this spring," Coco replied. "Maybe next year. I heard he's telling people he's training hard in swimming, but I think he wants to stay close to Mia. Madrid isn't Paris but at least they're on the same continent."

"I'm sorry to hear that," Haley said. "Things were always a little weird between me and Sebastian, but you can't say he wasn't stunning to look at."

"That's for sure."

Up ahead, Sasha was parking in front of L'Armoire. Coco parked a few spots away and waited for them to go in. Haley studied the area for the best possible secret shot setups.

"Let's shoot what we can through the store window first," she said to Coco. "Then go inside and see if we can lure him into saying something sweet about Linda."

"It won't take much, believe me," Coco said. "I was over at their house yesterday and Jonathan called her 'the light of my loins.' Twice."

"Ew," Haley said. "I'd rather catch something a little less graphic."

They walked up to the shop. Sasha and Jonathan were standing in front of a glass counter while a saleswoman showed them nightgowns. Haley shot a few frames through the window and they went inside.

A bell jingled as they opened the door, and Jonathan turned around. "Well, look who it is," Sasha said as if she'd had no idea Haley and Coco would walk in. "What are you guys doing here?"

"I'm all out of clear gloss," Coco said. "And I hate it when my lips are matte."

"So you can see we had to make an emergency stop," Haley added.

"That is a crisis," Jonathan said. He tried on a wide-brimmed sun hat. "What do you think of this as a little honeymoon gift for my sweet patootie?"

Haley nosed the camera lens out of her bag and shot what she could, hoping the picture was centered enough.

"She'll love it, Dad," Sasha said.

"It'll go great with her eyes," Coco said.

"Her eyes are brown, not blue," Jonathan said. "Brown as melted chocolate."

"That's what I mean," Coco said, recovering. "Blue offsets brown eyes really well."

"I'll take your word for it," Jonathan said. "Hmm, maybe I should pick up a little something for myself, too. Do you carry any sexy men's items?" he asked the saleswoman.

Haley thought she saw Sasha flinch at the question, and she didn't blame her. She couldn't imagine what a sexy men's item might be, but she hated to think of her own father in some kind of mesh banana hammock.

The saleswoman smiled uncomfortably. "Try a department store. For men, I always recommend a nice bathrobe."

Oh, thank God, Haley thought.

"Great idea," Jonathan said. "I'll get us matching his-and-hers robes."

"Shall I wrap this up?" the saleswoman asked, holding up the nightgown.

"Please do," Jonathan said. "And throw in a couple of pairs of these lacy panties."

The saleswoman wrapped up his purchases in pink tissue paper and put them in a shiny pink box with an elegant black bow.

"Thank you," Jonathan said. "Well, girls, we're off to the rest of the mall."

"Mind if we tag along?" Haley asked. "I just remembered I desperately need . . . uh . . . a pair of socks."

"Sure, the more the merrier," Sasha said brightly, as if it all hadn't been planned ahead of time.

Haley and Coco followed them to the department store, where Jonathan picked out royal blue velour his-and-hers bathrobes. "These are exactly what I was looking for. Linda will love this."

"I'm sorry, sir, but we're out of your size," the salesman said. "Someone just bought the last one. But we do have the ladies' robe in the size you wanted."

"Just the ladies' robe, then," Jonathan said. "I'll have to do without for now."

"We'll be getting more in next month," the salesman said. "Shall I have it monogrammed?"

"Thanks, that would be great," Jonathan said. He

turned to Sasha and asked, "Should I put her initials on the pocket, or her nickname?"

"What's her nickname?" Haley asked, unwisely, as it turned out.

"Snuggums," Jonathan said. "Well, that's one of her nicknames."

"Definitely her initials," Coco advised.

Haley's phone buzzed: a text coming in from Whitney. She pulled Sasha aside.

"Whitney and her mom are just walking into the mall—and they're headed for this department."

Sasha nodded. "I'll get Dad out of here. Did you catch the Snuggums bit on video?"

"Got it," Haley said. "Coco and I will go have an accidental meet-and-greet with Whitney."

"Dad, we've got a couple more stops to make," Sasha said to Jonathan. "We should get going."

"Nice to see you girls," Jonathan said, waving as Sasha dragged him out of loungewear.

"We got some 'his' footage," Haley told Coco. "Now to get the 'hers' side of things."

"I hope to God Linda Klein doesn't have any cute nicknames for Sasha's father," Coco said as they hurried toward the mall entrance. "I almost lost my lunch there for a minute."

As they rode down the escalator they passed Whitney and Linda going up. Whitney squealed with delight and fake surprise. "What are you guys *doing* here? Oh my God! That's so funny!"

Coco rolled her eyes. "As if I don't go to the mall at least three times a week."

"Come up and meet us in loungewear!" Whitney called as she glided out of sight.

At the bottom of the escalator Haley and Coco got off and turned around to go back up to loungewear. Haley was glad she was getting paid for this gig—it was turning out to be even less "artistic" than she'd expected.

When they reached loungewear, Linda Klein was putting a large box on the counter and explaining something to the salesman. "I bought this robe yesterday, but this morning I realized I wanted to have it monogrammed," she said. She pulled back the tissue paper to reveal the exact same blue velour robe that Jonathan had just bought for her. Haley and Coco exchanged knowing glances as Haley zoomed in on the robe. "It's for a very special occasion, so I want to make it as personal as possible."

"No problem, madam," the salesman said. "I can have it for you in a few days."

"Thank you."

Whitney opened another shopping bag, from L'Armoire. "Look at this negligee Mom got for her honeymoon. Isn't it beautiful?"

She revealed a pale blue lace nightgown—the same one Jonathan had just picked out to give to her.

"Do you think Jonnycakes will like it?" Linda asked.

"Jonnycakes?" Coco's face went green. Apparently this was a little more lovey-doveyness than she could handle in broad daylight.

"I'm one hundred percent positive he will," Haley said.

The next day Haley went to Whitney's house and secretly taped Linda as she arranged for champagne to be delivered to Jonathan's dressing room before the wedding ceremony. "And please include a nice card with this note," she instructed over the phone. "'To my darling Jonathan on this, the happiest day of my life. Thank you for making me whole again. All my love forever, Linda.' Have you got that? Good. Thank you!"

Two days later, Haley caught Jonathan sending a bottle of sparkling cider to Linda, only his note said, "Today we embark on a new adventure, where we become Snuggums and Jonnycakes for life. And what a wonderful life it will be!"

By the end of the week, Haley had plenty of video footage to show in sickening detail how well matched and in love Linda and Jon were. "It's almost eerie," she said to Sasha and Whitney at school one day. "They're like long-lost twins or something. They truly are a perfect match."

"See! We told you," Whitney said. "I can't wait for the wedding. It's so exciting I feel like I'm going to burst!"

"I can't wait to see your video," Sasha said. "When will it be ready?"

"I need a few days to edit it," Haley said. "I want to make it as effective as possible."

"Perfect," Sasha said. "When they see this at the rehearsal dinner they're going to be bawling into their spaghetti carbonara."

"I hope so," Haley said. "If bawling in spaghetti is a good thing."

"It definitely is," Whitney said.

● ● ●

Haley's first job as a professional filmmaker seems to be going well, even if it's not her ideal assignment. She'll find a way to take all that icky sentiment and show the real love behind it. That's the challenge, anyway, and Haley hopes she's up to it.

But as heartwarming as Whitney and Sasha's world of wedding prep is, has Haley had enough of it? Once she's finished with the video, should she stick around to help her friends get ready for the big day? Or should Haley back away and focus on another area of her life—schoolwork, perhaps? Maybe schoolwork combined with an extremely hot guy?

If you think Haley should stay in wedding world for a while, send her to WK STUDIO on page 98. If you think she needs a study break—and a little masculine companionship—go to page 84, STUDY WITH REESE.

FOUR DRESSES

Trust a mother to come through at those big moments.

Haley had a feeling, when her mother knocked lightly on her bedroom door, that something good was coming. Usually her mother stopped by to check on how her homework was going, or to update Haley on her work schedule for the week, or to complain that Haley hadn't emptied the dishwasher as promised. But the look on Joan Miller's face just then said "special mother-daughter moment," so Haley sat up and said, "Come in."

"The prom's coming up, isn't it?" Joan said, sitting beside Haley on her bed.

"It sure is," Haley said. She crossed her fingers, hoping Joan would offer to buy her a dress. Haley had saved up some money to buy one herself, but with Joan's help she could get something really special.

Joan drew out the suspense. Sometimes she liked to make Haley wait for good news. "I remember my junior prom," she said. "I have to admit, it wasn't exactly the evening I'd dreamed of. I liked this boy named Eric, but he asked my best friend, Frannie, instead of me, so I ended up going with this guy I didn't know so well who drove a van. A metallic blue van lined with shag carpeting."

Haley laughed. "You went to the prom in a van?"

"It was a classic. It had a very loud motor and flames airbrushed along the side. And the only music you ever heard coming out of it was Van Halen."

"Mom, were you a metalhead in high school?" Haley had never heard this story before—it seemed to be a memory her mother had tried to repress.

"No! Not at all," Joan said. "I was a social-protest nerd. That's what made going to the prom with Neil Cordero so painful for me."

"But you went," Haley said.

"I went, and Neil was actually very nice. Eric was the jerk. He was all over Frannie all night. Neil caught me looking over at them and guessed what was going on, so instead of suffering through the all-night afterparty, he offered to take me out for ice cream."

"Mom! That's sweet."

"It was sweet, now that I look back on it. But at the time I just felt miserable. I didn't want ice cream, I wanted romance. And not with a guy in a van."

"What about your senior prom?" Haley asked.

"That was much nicer," Joan said. "By then I'd been going out with this boy named Harris Stapleton for almost a year, so I didn't have to go on an awkward date or anything. I was already in love. Or, well, not love, exactly, but I liked him a lot."

"What did you wear?"

"I wore this very pretty white eyelet dress with an off-the-shoulder ruffle . . . simple and sweet. I've seen dresses just like it in the stores lately. That's what I wanted to talk to you about. Have you decided what kind of dress you'd like to wear to your prom?"

"Not yet," Haley said. "I thought I'd wait and see what kind of price range I'd be working with first."

Joan patted her fondly. "That's my good sensible girl. Listen—don't worry about that. I want to give you a dress for your prom. Okay?"

Haley grinned. "Okay."

"The way I see it, you have four options. One,

you can wear my old white eyelet prom dress. I just had it dry cleaned and it looks beautiful. It's hanging on my closet door if you want to see it."

Haley got up to go to her parents' room, and her mother followed. The white dress hung in a protective plastic sleeve. "Try it on if you like," Joan said. "I think it will fit you."

"It's cute," Haley said. It didn't look dated at all. Her mother was right—dresses just like this were all over the mall.

"But don't feel you have to wear that dress just to please me," Joan said. "You've got three other options. You could look for a different dress at the vintage store, if this one isn't your style. Or we could see what they've got at Mimi's." Mimi's Boutique was a chic dress shop housed in a renovated Dairy Queen. "Or if you've got something special in mind and want something unique, we could have Whitney custom-make a new dress for you."

Whitney Klein had started her own dress business, WK, and was doing very well. She was definitely talented, and could make anything Haley wanted and fit it exactly to her figure.

"That's a lot of options," Haley said. "It's a tough choice."

"Think about it," Joan said, kissing her on the forehead. "Whatever you decide is fine with me. I just want you to be happy."

"Thanks, Mom." Haley was genuinely touched

by her mother's generous offer. She and Joan didn't always get along, but when it came right down to it Haley had to admit she had two awesome parents.

"One thing, though," Joan said. "If you come here and tell me you're going to the prom in a van, the deal's off."

Haley laughed. "Don't worry—there's no danger of that."

"Good."

●　●　●

Joan Miller's generous offer leads to a dilemma for Haley: exactly what kind of dress *does* she want? She doesn't know who her prom date will be yet. The problem is really to decide what kind of person she is, or wants to be. Is she a sweet, traditional girl in her mother's hand-me-down prom dress? Or does she want a funkier vintage vibe? Should she take the easy way out with a dress from Mimi's, sure to be elegant and chic, or be really creative and have Whitney make something just for her?

If you think Haley should wear Joan's prom dress, go to page 84, STUDY WITH REESE. If you think she should shop for the prom at Jack's Vintage Clothing, go to page 107, BANQUET ROOM. If you think Haley is mature enough now to pull off an elegant prom gown, go to page 91, STUDY WITH ALEX. And if you think she should refract her prom image through Whitney's designing eyes, go to page 98, WK STUDIO.

Choose carefully: the prom is a terrible thing to waste.

A kid sister can bring out
the best in a guy.

"Lower," Mitchell called out. "Lower!"

Haley was pushing him on the swings in River-vale Park. "Don't you mean 'higher'?" she asked, pushing him more gently this time. "Most kids want to go higher."

"No. Lower," Mitchell said. So Haley pushed even more gently, until his swing made a low arc over the muddy, dried grass under the swing set. Mitchell hadn't been going that high in the first place. Haley had never heard of a kid asking to go lower. It seemed weird.

"Swing next to me," Mitchell said. "I can pump my legs myself."

Haley sat down in the next swing and rocked back and forth beside him. Maybe wanting to go lower wasn't such a weird sign after all. Maybe Mitchell just wanted to talk.

Haley suddenly realized that she had only one year left at home before she went off—somewhere, she didn't know where yet—to college. By then Mitchell would still be only nine years old, with almost a decade to spend home alone with their parents. She'd decided to pay more attention to Mitchell from now on, and if she didn't have a lot of free time to spend with him, at least to make it count.

"What's on your mind, Mitchie?" Haley asked.

"I'm sad."

Haley was touched. Mitchell had trouble expressing his feelings through words—his usual method was through taking things apart or smashing things—so this seemed like a major breakthrough. *Wow,* Haley thought. *I spend ten minutes alone with him and already he's opening up to me. Maybe I should become a child psychologist instead of a filmmaker. Or maybe I could do both.* Her next film project could be a study of Mitchell, or of little kids in general: what their inner lives were really like, what they did when they thought no one was looking.

"What are you sad about?" she asked, bringing her focus back to her brother.

"I miss RoBro!" Mitchell said.

Haley sighed. RoBro! was a robot brother that Haley's classmate Dave Metzger had built. Dave was a geeky, lonely only child whose father had abandoned him. He treated RoBro! like a real brother, and when RoBro!'s circuits snapped, he'd called on electronics prodigy Mitchell to help save him. Haley hadn't realized that Mitchell had gotten so attached to RoBro! Did he need a mechanical brother too? Now *that* was sad.

Haley thought she probably should have started paying more attention to Mitchell a long time ago.

"Mitchell, RoBro! is cool and everything, but he's not a real person. He's just a robot. Kind of like a doll. If you want, I could get you a toy robot and you could pretend he's RoBro!"

Mitchell shook his head. "It's not the same. RoBro! was real. He could talk! Dave thought he was real. Remember how Dave cried when RoBro! was sick?"

How could she forget? The sight of Dave Metzger crying was the kind of thing you couldn't get out of your head no matter how hard you tried.

"Well, I haven't seen RoBro! in a while, but I'm sure Dave will let you visit him whenever you want," she told Mitchell. "After all, you"—she swallowed, wondering if what she was about to say was a good idea, since it would only encourage Mitchell's illusion that RoBro! was alive—"saved his life."

78

"Okay," Mitchell said, dragging his feet in the muddy dirt under his swing. "That would be good."

"But maybe you don't need RoBro! so much," Haley added. "Because you have me."

He glanced at her warily under pale brown bangs that needed trimming. "You're always busy."

"I know," Haley said. "But I'm going to try to spend more time with you when I can. Okay?"

"Yeah. Okay."

The April weather was still chilly, and the park was quiet. Haley looked up when she heard the sound of wheels on pavement. Devon rolled into sight on his skateboard, followed by his little sister, Shana, on her scooter.

"It's Shana," Mitchell said. He knew her from school, and his face brightened at the sight of her. Haley herself couldn't help feeling a little relieved to have some company.

Shana scooted over to the swings. She was a pretty little girl, pale and delicate. "Want to try my scooter?" she asked Mitchell.

Mitchell nodded shyly and jumped off the swing. The two of them chased each other on the scooter. Devon flipped his skateboard into the air and caught it in one hand. Then he sat down in the empty swing next to Haley.

"'Sup," he said.

"Just doing my big-sister thing," Haley said. "What are you two doing so far from home?"

Devon lived in the Floods, on the other side of town from Haley's neighborhood bordering the affluent Heights. He usually took Shana to Bailey Park in the Floods—Rivervale Park was pretty far out of his way. *He must still be in heavy Darcy-avoidance mode to come all the way over here just to go to the playground,* she thought, not without satisfaction.

"We needed a change of scene," Devon said. "Shana gets tired of the same old seesaw. And I'm glad we came, because now she has someone to play with."

"Mitchell's happy to see her, too," Haley said.

"Working on any new video projects these days?" Devon asked.

"I've had an interesting offer," Haley said, remembering Whitney Klein's and Sasha Lewis's constant calls begging her to make a video to commemorate their parents' upcoming wedding.

"Your film inspired me to quit procrastinating and start working on a project I've had in mind for a while," he said.

"Oh yeah?" Haley crossed her legs and kicked one foot lightly up and down, her eyes on the toe of her scuffed brown boot. "What's that?"

"Formal portraits," he said. "Photographs, of course, in full color, very saturated and very deliberately posed. Like portraits of royalty, except I want to show regular people—waitresses, janitors, high school kids—in a dignified setting, so that the line between parody and seriousness is blurred."

"Sounds interesting," Haley said. "Where is all this happening?"

"That was the first big problem I had," Devon said. "Setting is crucial, and I wanted a place with a certain kind of gaudy grandeur—"

"What about the governor's mansion?" Haley suggested. "Maybe Spencer would give you permission to shoot in the grand ballroom."

Devon smirked. "You're joking, right? Anyway, that's not gaudy enough, not in the populist way I'm looking for. We're shooting at the Golden Dynasty, in the banquet room, on Monday."

Haley laughed. The Golden Dynasty was a Chinese restaurant owned by Irene's parents, and the banquet room was a symphony in red and gold and bamboo, complete with a gigantic fish tank. "That's gaudy, all right. And perfect. How did you get Mr. Chen to let you do that?"

"Basically I begged Irene to beg him. And he actually said yes. I think she might have had to make some kind of pact with the devil regarding her SAT scores, but it worked."

"Sounds like an amazing project," Haley said.

"Why don't you come by and check it out?" Devon suggested. "I was thinking the whole thing might be even cooler if we added a video component.

Like, while I'm shooting the still portraits, you could interview the subjects, kind of like you did in San Francisco. And maybe film the process of taking the photographs, choosing the outfits, posing people and putting them at ease . . . all that stuff. What do you think?"

Haley thought it sounded fascinating. The only trouble was, she had a lot of studying to do, especially for the big AP History test coming up, and she didn't have time for everything.

● ● ●

Everyone seems to want in on the Haley video express. She's impressed a lot of people with her skills and talent, that's clear. And it must be nice to get some positive attention from Devon for a change. Ever since he saw her video, he seems to respect and admire her—and possibly be romantically interested. It's hard to tell for sure with an intense guy like Devon. He takes his artwork very seriously, and that may be the only kind of collaboration he wants with Haley. Or not. A lot of artistic collaborations turn into personal relationships. It's not a given, but it is a natural progression.

Still, Devon's not the only boy who admires Haley for her talents. Alex Martin thinks she has the makings of a brilliant historian. Haley could ace AP History if she tried—but that means studying and studying hard. Alex aced the class last year, aced the AP exam and got into a hot school like Georgetown—he's Haley's ideal tutor.

But would she rather focus her energies on her brainy side or her artistic side?

If you think Haley should join Devon at Golden Dynasty to shoot art portraits, go to page 107, BANQUET ROOM. If you think Haley should worry more about her upcoming AP History test, go to page 91, STUDY WITH ALEX.

No one's saying a girl can't be artistic *and* brainy. But when the crush of junior year comes down on her head, a girl's got to make some choices, or go crazy trying.

When a smart boy plays dumb, you know he likes you.

"Do you get this part about the Archduke Ferdinand?" Reese asked Haley. "I mean, Serbia's this tiny country. How could it start World War One?"

Haley sat next to Reese on the couch in the basement of the Highlands' house, studying for the upcoming AP History test. Their history textbooks were splayed out on the coffee table in front of them, open to the chapter on World War I, along with a big bowl of cheese doodles. Haley enjoyed munching on the cheese doodles, which were something she never got in her superorganic, sugar-free home.

"We went over this," Haley said.

"I know," Reese said. "But you so nailed it in class the other day. I want to hear your take on it."

"The Serbs were afraid that the Austrians were going to take over Serbia, so one of them assassinated the Austrian heir to the throne. Which gave the Austrians the excuse they were looking for to invade." She was a little suspicious of Reese's question, since he was a history whiz and she was pretty sure he'd explained the whole Franz Ferdinand situation to her an hour or so earlier. She suspected him of trying to prolong their study session and having his mind more on her than on history. "So the Russians freaked out that the Austrians were going to start heading east and gobbling up countries left and right to threaten them, and then the Germans jumped in to help Austria, which freaked out the French . . ."

"Ah, France." Reese practically batted his eyelashes at her. She had to admit they were very nice lashes. "Good food, good perfume, good lingerie . . ."

"Why do boys always have longer lashes than girls?" Haley asked. "It's not fair."

"Because we're hairier," Reese said. "Eyelashes are hair." He leaned forward and brushed his long eyelashes against her arm.

"Keep your mind on your work," Haley scolded playfully.

"I can't," Reese said, lounging back on the couch. "It's spring! I have spring fever."

Haley glanced out the basement window, where the ground was being pelted with gray rain. "It's fifty degrees out and pouring. Not exactly picnic weather."

"You know what they say: April showers bring May flowers."

"Which are picked in June to make prom corsages and bridal bouquets," Haley said.

"Proms and weddings," Reese said thoughtfully. "I know of some proms and weddings coming up. One of each, actually."

"I know of two weddings," Haley said. "And they're both on the same day."

"The Sasha-Whitney wedding," Reese said. By "Sasha-Whitney," Reese meant Sasha Lewis's father and Whitney Klein's mother, of course. "And what else?"

"Mr. Von and Mrs. Metzger." Übergeek Dave Metzger's mother, Nora, was engaged to Rick Von, the popular but odd Hillsdale art teacher, and Dave had invited much of Hillsdale's brainy crowd.

"Oh, right! Someone actually agreed to marry Mr. Von. I didn't realize that was the same day. Are you going to the Klein-Lewis bash? I can't wait to see Sasha and Whitney joined in holy stepsisterhood."

"I'd love to see that too," Haley said. "But I haven't decided which wedding to go to yet."

"You were invited to both? Aren't you Miss Popular."

Haley was a little taken aback by Reese's teasing tone; it was unusual for him to be so jovial and flirty. Normally he was very focused and goal-oriented, especially during a study session. She wondered what had gotten into him. Maybe it really was spring fever.

"I think it would mean a lot to Dave if I went to his mother's wedding," she said. "He's so socially awkward and so . . . emotionally fragile. He's the kind of guy who takes things personally, you know? That's why I was thinking I might have to make an appearance there. I don't want to hurt his feelings."

"But he'll have Annie and Hannah and those other brainiacs to keep him company," Reese said.

"That's the other thing that's bothering me," Haley said. "Have you noticed anything weird between Dave and Annie?" Annie Armstrong had been Dave's girlfriend for over a year now, and they'd always seemed like one of the tightest couples at school. But lately Haley had noticed signs of wear and tear. They didn't sit together in the courtyard on warm days, and didn't hold hands when walking down the halls.

"I haven't noticed anything, but then they're not exactly on my radar," Reese said.

"It worries me. I hate to think they might break up just when his mother remarries. That would crush Dave. Did you know he actually looked up his biological father, but when he went to visit him his father rejected him?"

"Wow. That's rough."

"It crushed Dave," Haley said. "I guess that's why I feel sort of an obligation to support him. But on the other hand, the Lewis-Klein wedding sounds like a lot of fun."

"It's going to be way more fun," Reese said. "That's the one you should go to. All your real friends will be there, like Coco—"

Haley laughed at the idea of Coco being anybody's "real" friend.

"—and of course Sasha and Whitney. And then there's me. I'm going to be there."

He leaned so close to her she could smell the cheese doodles on his breath.

"We're supposed to be studying," Haley said. She was flattered by his flirting, but at the same time, she'd come over determined to master the first half of twentieth-century European history, and they couldn't seem to get past 1914.

"I know. But I'm making it my mission to make sure you go to the wedding. If you're not there, how will I entertain myself?"

"I'm sure you'll figure something out," Haley said.

"I bet they'll have great food, and a band, and it will be a beautiful night, and all the cool people in town will be there—if you don't go you'll kick yourself for missing it."

"Maybe so," Haley said. "But if I don't go to Mr. Von's wedding I could miss out on some spectacular weirdness. Which might be useful as an artist. And what if Dave gets so upset that his friends aren't at the wedding that he has some kind of breakdown? I don't want to be responsible for that."

"You shouldn't be," Reese said. "You're not responsible for Dave's mental health. That's too much to ask of a pretty girl like you."

Haley shook her head and tapped her pen on the textbook. "Reese—the Archduke Ferdinand?"

"Oh, right. Right. It's just so hard to concentrate around you these days. . . ."

● ● ●

Wow, Reese is really pouring it on. Haley is flattered, but falling for flattery doesn't fit into her plan to be newly focused and serious this year. Though maybe she could use a little fun.

She knows Reese is right about one thing: the Lewis-Klein wedding will be the place to be that weekend. If she misses it, she'll be missing the social event of the year. She'll also be missing a chance at a romantic evening with Reese, if his heavy-handed hinting means anything. It could be a night she'll remember forever.

But if the Lewis-Klein wedding appeals to her social side, the Metzger-Von wedding appeals to the quirky part of Haley. It's true she doesn't want to hurt Dave's feelings, but she also can't help being deeply curious about what is going to happen when two oddballs mate for life. The brainy crowd will probably be there to help her enjoy the spectacle. And someone else Haley's interested in is likely to be there too: Alex Martin, the supersmart senior. This could be Haley's chance to move things forward with Alex, if she's interested.

Of course, whichever wedding she chooses to go to will cause hurt feelings in the friend she leaves out. Dave's more likely to lose it if she doesn't show up to support him in his hour of need, but Sasha and Whitney will surely be offended as well if she turns down their invitation. For Sasha and Whitney, the wedding of their parents is not just a wedding but the formation of a completely new family, and the transition of their relationship from friendship to sisterhood. They're primed to celebrate, and want all their friends there celebrating with them.

So perhaps Haley should cut her losses and turn down both invitations. Both parties will be disappointed, but neither one will be able to say Haley dissed them for the other.

If you think Haley shouldn't miss the wedding of the year, turn to page 118, LEWIS-KLEIN WEDDING. If you think she'd be a fool to miss Dave's reaction to the union of his mother and Mr. Von, turn to page 138, METZGER-VON WEDDING. If you think Haley should avoid offending anyone and turn down both invitations, turn to page 132, STAY HOME.

Can great dates in history lead to great dates in romance?

"You've got World War One down cold." Alex playfully bumped his elbow against Haley's. They were sitting at the dining room table in his parents' ultratraditional colonial house, with his mother, Mary, in the kitchen making dinner and not-so-subtly eavesdropping on them. Alex didn't seem to be aware of the way his mother cocked an ear toward them every time they mentioned something she might find interesting—the word *date,* for example, which came up a lot in history discussions, though not in the way Mary Martin seemed to hope or fear. But Haley was keenly tuned in and tried to be careful what she allowed Mrs. Martin to overhear. There was a tight network of mothers in Hillsdale, and they talked.

"Good," Haley said. "So what's next?"

"On to the Roaring Twenties, the Great Depression and the lead-up to World War Two," Alex said. "Let's go over some crucial dates."

Mrs. Martin suddenly stopped peppering the flank steak and leaned toward the dining room. Haley almost burst out laughing. Alex was totally oblivious.

"We've got March 1938—" he prompted.

"Hitler's army marches into Austria," Haley replied. "I always remember that from *The Sound of Music*."

"December seventh, 1941—"

"Japanese planes attack Pearl Harbor."

"Good. January 1943."

"Tough one." Haley paused to rack through her memory, and then it came to her. "The Russians defeat the German army outside Stalingrad. These are kind of arbitrary dates."

Mrs. Martin nearly dropped the cup of flour she was carrying to the stove.

"I know," Alex said. "But you're rocking them. I just thought I'd give you a little pop quiz to see what we need to work on. Certainly not dates." Haley glanced into the kitchen in time to catch Mrs. Martin's head popping up from behind the refrigerator door. "Maybe essay questions."

Mrs. Martin stepped into the dining room. "Do you kids need anything? Dinner won't be ready for an hour, Alex, so I can fix you a plate of carrot sticks or something if you're hungry."

Alex glanced at Haley, who nodded her head. "Sounds great."

"And will you be staying for dinner, Haley?" she asked.

"Thanks, but no," Haley said. "I should probably go home soon."

Haley had come home from school with Alex at three and hadn't expected to spend so many hours studying with him. But he was such a good tutor and so knowledgeable about history. He was also quite cute and a very nice guy. The time flew by and she hardly felt as if she were studying at all.

"Sure? We'd love to have you and there's plenty of food."

Haley was tempted—they rarely ate steak in the Miller household, for numerous nutritional and environmental reasons—but she was afraid of spending too much time with Alex and overstaying her welcome.

"I can't," she said. "We're having Tofu Surprise tonight—wouldn't want to miss that."

Mrs. Martin looked mystified by this answer, but Alex laughed. His little brothers, Calvin and

Christian, rolled into the dining room on scooters, chasing each other around the table.

"No scooters in the house, boys!" their mother scolded. "How many times have I told you?"

They scooted away, laughing while she chased after them. Haley was relieved to have a brief moment of privacy with Alex at last. She happened to notice a stack of mail on the table, with a fancy envelope from Nora Metzger on top. She picked it up.

"Are you going to Mrs. Metzger's wedding?" she asked Alex. Dave Metzger's mother, Nora, was engaged to Hillsdale art teacher Rick Von. The engagement had shaken Dave up a bit.

He nodded. "How about you? It should be interesting, if nothing else."

"I haven't decided yet," Haley replied.

Alex laughed. "Why, do you have something better to do?"

"Actually, I was invited to another wedding on the same day," Haley revealed. "Sasha Lewis's dad and Whitney Klein's mom."

"I heard they were getting married," Alex said. "Too bad it has to be the same day. And you were invited to both! But you're going to the Metzger bash, right?"

"It's so hard to decide," Haley complained. "I know his mom's wedding is a big deal for Dave, but Sasha and Whitney are about to become stepsisters, and that's a big deal to them too."

"Weddings are always a big deal for the people involved," Alex said. His mother suddenly reappeared, flushed from chasing her younger sons around.

"Wedding? Did I hear the word 'wedding'?"

"We were just talking about Mrs. Metzger and Mr. Von," Alex said.

"Oh." Mrs. Martin looked relieved. "Did you remember to send in your RSVP for that, Alex?"

"Yes, Mom. I was just trying to talk Haley into going too."

"She can't go if she wasn't invited," Mrs. Martin said.

"She was invited," Alex said. "But she was also invited to another wedding and she can't decide which one to go to."

"Linda Klein's wedding?" Mrs. Martin asked. Haley nodded. "A friend of mine told me all about that situation. They met in AA or someplace like that, didn't they?"

"I think so," Haley said.

"Not the soundest basis for a marriage, I wouldn't think," Mrs. Martin sniffed. "But who am I to judge?"

"You never know what really goes on between two people in love," Haley said.

Mrs. Martin arched an eyebrow. "What a mature thing for a girl your age to say."

"I've heard my mother say it a million times," Haley said. "Not that I'd know anything like that from experience."

"I should hope not."

"Hey, Mom, could you get us those carrot sticks now?" Alex said, clearly tired of his mother's snooping.

"Yes, sweetie, I'll be back in a minute." She swept out of the dining room. Haley was suddenly struck by how neatly dressed Mrs. Martin was for someone cooking dinner—an apron over neat wool slacks and a ribbed turtleneck sweater, not a spot on her.

"Sorry about that," Alex said. "My mom can be a little rigid sometimes."

"That's okay," Haley said. "My mother humiliates me on a regular basis. Why do you think I told you I'd rather study here than at my house?"

They shared a laugh over the ridiculousness of mothers. Then Alex said, "Seriously, Haley, I hope you'll go to the Metzger-Von wedding. We could have fun together. I'll save the first dance for you. And the last. And any dances you might want in between."

Haley couldn't resist a glance at the kitchen doorway, where Mrs. Martin stood frozen in place, the plate of carrots in her hands and a look of dismay on her even features. Did Alex's mother want Haley to say yes or no to Alex's request? Haley couldn't tell.

● ● ●

Haley faces a real dilemma here. If she goes to Dave's mom's wedding she'll make Dave very happy, and from the way things are sounding, Alex too. But then she'll

have to miss the Lewis-Klein wedding, and Sasha and Whitney will be upset, maybe even angry. Haley assumes that Reese Highland will be at the Lewis-Klein shindig, which could be interesting as well.

But if she tries to please Sasha and Whitney by going to *their* nuptial bash, Dave's feelings will surely be hurt. And Alex's. What's a girl to do?

She could stay neutral and refuse to go to either wedding. That way she'd avoid hurting a lot of people's feelings, but she might also miss out on a lot of fun.

Instead of worrying about pleasing everyone else in town, the real question that Haley needs to answer is this: what does *she* want?

If you think Haley wants to dance with Alex at the **METZGER-VON WEDDING**, turn to page 138. If you think Haley wants to whoop it up at the **LEWIS-KLEIN WEDDING**, turn to page 118. Finally, if you think Haley can't bear to choose and would rather just **STAY HOME**, turn to page 132.

Pre-wedding jitters can be very contagious.

"**D**oes anybody have any gum?" Whitney Klein shrieked. "Come on, people, somebody around here must have a lousy piece of gum!"

Haley walked into the WK design studio and found herself in the center of a chaotic whirlwind. Whitney was knee-deep in dress patterns and silk dupioni fabric and surrounded by fitting dummies of varying sizes, her mouth full of straight pins. Sasha posed half-naked on a fitting platform, wrapped in a swatch of stiff silk. Behind her stood a large easel with a design pad open to a drawing of a brides-maid's dress. Cecily was flipping through a look book, and Coco was holding a fashion magazine open to one particular spread and glaring at Whitney, while a UPS guy stood in the doorway impatiently waiting for Whitney to sign for a large box.

"Keep your panties on," Cecily said, dropping the look book to dig through her designer bag. "I might have some gum in here somewhere. . . ."

"Miss, could you sign for the delivery, please?" the UPS guy said. "I've got a lot of other stops to make today."

"I'm coming!" Whitney snapped. "Sasha, don't move!" She snatched the scanner from the UPS guy and signed it. That was when she noticed Haley hovering in the doorway, slightly afraid to cross the threshold.

"You might as well come in, Haley," Whitney said. "It's too crowded in here already. One more body won't make a difference."

"I was hoping you might make me a prom dress," Haley said. "But I can see you're pretty busy—"

"Busy!" Whitney cried. "I'm drowning. Between Mom's wedding dress, bridesmaids' dresses for me and Sasha, a dress for my aunt Laurie and prom dresses for half the girls in Hillsdale, I'm getting carpal tunnel. My hands are practically crippled from working, like, fifty hours a day."

"There are only twenty-four hours in a day,

Whit," Cecily reminded her, handing her a piece of gum. "Here's some sugarless."

"Sugarless! Bleh! I need sugar, and I need it now!"

Haley had never seen Whitney so wound up, and it worried her. Usually Whitney was spacey and dippy—maybe she was in over her head with this design business. "I can come back later if you want—"

"No, stay," Whitney said, draping the silk over Sasha's shoulders. "Prom is after Mom's wedding, so I'll have time to make you a dress then, if you don't mind waiting."

"That sounds great," Haley said.

"Who are you going with?" Cecily asked.

"I'm not sure yet," Haley replied. "You're lucky you have your date nailed down." Cecily was going with her boyfriend, Drew Napolitano. "I figure I'll go by myself if no one asks me."

"Someone will ask you for sure," Sasha said.

"Are you going with Johnny?" Cecily asked Sasha.

Sasha sighed. "I don't know. I can't decide whether or not to get back together with him."

"You might as well," Coco said. "You've hooked up with him the last three weekends in a row."

Haley was surprised to hear this. Coco, Cecily and Sasha had had a furious falling-out with their boyfriends when they found photos of them cavorting in the Caribbean with swimsuit models over winter break. But after a couple of months of freezing the boys out, Coco had relented and gone back with Spencer Eton, and Cecily had given in to the fact that she and Drew were meant to be. Sasha was the hold-out. Her relationship with Johnny Lane had always been rocky, but it sounded as if things were smoothing out between them.

"Has Spencer asked you yet, Coco?" Sasha asked.

"Not yet, but he *will*," Coco said. "It's still early, and you know how Spencer is—everything has to be spontaneous. Now that I'm a regular overnight guest at the governor's mansion, it's a foregone conclusion."

Spencer Eton's mother, Eleanor, was the newly elected governor of New Jersey, which went a long way toward helping Coco to forgive Spencer's little faults—which weren't so little. Haley knew he could be selfish, thoughtless, a drinker and a shameless flirt. But Coco could forgive all that in exchange for the glamour of the governor's mansion.

"I'm first in line for prom dresses," Coco said. "Whitney, you promised to have mine ready early, remember?"

"Don't worry, Coco—I've already drawn up something really elegant for you," Whitney said.

Coco fingered the silk fabric at Sasha's feet. "Well, I hope you're not planning on using this dupioni crap for my dress. It has no give at all!"

"This fabric costs thirty dollars a yard," Whitney said.

"I don't care if it costs a million dollars a yard, I want silk georgette," Coco said.

"But georgette is so tricky to sew," Whitney complained. "And the dress I designed for you works best in crepe de chine."

"Crepe de chine! Ugh! Where is this design of yours?" Coco began to flip through the drawing pad on the easel.

"It's the one with your name on it," Whitney said. She stuck a pin in the fabric near Sasha's shoulder.

"Ow!" Sasha cried. "Careful, Whit!"

"Sorry. Cecily, have you picked out a pattern for your prom dress yet?"

"There are so many good ones, it's hard to decide," Cecily said. "How do you think I'd look in this?" She held up a picture of a fitted, simple dress with a flower pattern. Coco turned her head to look.

"Like one of the kids in *The Sound of Music* when they're wearing those drapes," she said.

"I could make it in a solid color," Whitney said. "You'd look amazing in cherry red. Haley, do you know what kind of dress you have in mind?"

"I think I'll look through one of these idea books for a while," Haley said. She hadn't given it a lot of thought, just that she wanted something unique and stylish, and she knew Whitney could pull that off if she didn't lose her mind first.

Coco turned to a page showing a sketch of a flowing white lace gown. "Is this mine? I love this," she said.

"No, that's my mom's wedding dress."

"Can you make the same thing for me in seafoam?" Coco asked.

"My mom would kill me," Whitney said.

"Coco, that's totally not cool," Sasha added.

Coco grunted with dissatisfaction and kept turning the pages until she came to a sketch marked *Coco*.

"What?" she screeched. "No. You have got to be kidding me!"

Cecily, Haley and Sasha turned to look at the sketch. It showed a sleeveless teal-blue dress with a jeweled V-neck and long, slightly flared skirt.

"Come on, Coco, that's beautiful," Sasha said.

"It's garbage," Coco said, clearly in "Coco the Hun" mode. "Teal? What am I, a walking dentist's office?"

"That was just an idea," Whitney said. "I can make it any color you want."

"What about this tacky jeweled neckline?" Coco stabbed a finger at the page. "Could it be any more last year?"

"Jeweled necklines are pretty timeless," Whitney protested weakly.

"Like you'd know," Coco said. "What is it, Whitney? Are you jealous of me? Are you trying to sabotage my prom night by making me hideous?"

"Coco, you could never be hideous. . . ."

Haley hated to see Whitney revert to her old insecure beta-girl habits with Coco. Since she and Sasha had become closer, Whitney had gotten more confident, but every once in a while Coco could bring out the quivering mouse in Whitney.

"No. This is unacceptable." Coco picked up a red marker and slashed a bloody *X* through the sketch. "Start over, Whitney. And this time try to come up with something a person might wear this century."

"What are you going to wear to the wedding, Haley?" Sasha asked. Haley figured Sasha was trying to help out Whitney by changing the subject.

"Oh, um, I haven't decided yet," Haley said. Actually, she hadn't decided for sure if she was even going to the Lewis-Klein wedding. She'd also been invited to witness the marriage of Dave Metzger's mother to Mr. Rick Von, the art teacher, which was taking place the very same day. Haley had been leaning toward going to Whitney and Sasha's big event, but the tense scene at WK was making her reconsider.

"Wear something sexy," Cecily advised. "Everybody who's anybody is going to be there, including most of the cutest boys in town."

"One of them might be inspired to ask you to the

prom while dancing with you at the wedding," Sasha added.

"I don't think we've gotten your RSVP yet, have we?" Whitney said. "You should send it in soon. The caterer wants the final head count next week."

"Okay," Haley said, her stomach flipping nervously. "I'll be sure to do that."

● ● ●

The time has come for Haley to make up her mind about this wedding situation. The Lewis-Klein wedding seems like an obvious choice at first—all Haley's friends will be there, as well as the hottest guys in town, as Cecily pointed out. There are a lot to choose from, from bad boy Matt Graham to good guy Reese Highland. A girl could do worse.

But seeing the state the wedding prep has put Whitney in might remind Haley why she sometimes likes to linger on the edge of this particular clique. When it comes right down to it, at the highest level of social life at Hillsdale High, Coco rules, and what she wants preempts everything. An independent girl like Haley could find that tiresome.

And the Metzger-Von wedding could be interesting, especially appealing to Haley's artistic side. Mr. Von is her art teacher, after all, and known for his eccentricity. If she could get permission to videotape the party, she might get some amazing footage. But even if she doesn't record the event on video, it could stir her imagination and give her ideas for her future work. Besides, the brainy Dave Metzger–Annie Armstrong crowd has its strong points—like adorable Alex Martin, who is sure to be at the wedding.

If you think Haley should go to the LEWIS-KLEIN WEDDING, go to page 118. If you think she should geek out at the METZGER-VON WEDDING, go to page 138. If you think all this decision-making is giving her a headache and she'd rather opt out of the whole situation, have her STAY HOME on page 132.

BANQUET ROOM

A portrait sometimes reveals more about the artist than about the subject.

"Let's try that gray partition as a backdrop." Devon pointed to a carpeted wall divider in the banquet room at Golden Dynasty restaurant. Shaun and Irene picked it up and moved it against the back wall. The rest of the room was painted red and gold and decorated with Chinese paper lanterns. It was the height of kitsch, which, Haley thought, was just what Devon liked about it.

"Great," Devon said. He adjusted his camera on its tripod and peered into the viewer. "That's about the right distance. Okay, I think I'd like to shoot Kiki first. Is she ready?"

"I'll go check." Irene ran into the ladies' room, which was doubling as a dressing room for the subjects of Devon's photo project. Irene's father had agreed to let Devon use the banquet room as a set on Monday afternoon, when the restaurant was slow, and Irene and Shaun had volunteered to help set up the shoot and corral some of the restaurant employees into posing for pictures. Haley was videotaping the proceedings and interviewing the portrait subjects. She and Devon thought they might try to get a show together, combining still and video portraits.

Kiki, one of the waitresses, appeared in the costume Devon had chosen for her: a black tuxedo with turquoise bow tie and matching cummerbund. Devon worked at Jack's Vintage Clothing shop, so he had access to all kinds of funky outfits.

"This is really what you want me to wear?" Kiki asked. "I look ridiculous."

"You look fantastic," Devon said, peering at her through the viewfinder as she stood in front of the partition. "Irene, can I get a little more eye shadow? Make that a lot more."

Irene daubed turquoise eye shadow over Kiki's dark eyes, then touched up her ruby lipstick. "All set."

Haley turned on her video camera and zoomed in

on Kiki. "Okay, Kiki. While Devon shoots your portrait, I'm going to ask you a few questions. You don't have to answer anything you're not comfortable with. Okay?"

"This is the weirdest day off from work I've had in a long time," Kiki said. Haley took that as an okay.

"Wait," Devon said. "Kiki, I know this sounds funny, but you look too relaxed. I want you to pose stiffly, like you feel self-conscious. Straight back, chin up, arms by your sides." He walked over to pose her the way he wanted her. "I want these portraits to look very formal, like paintings. Pretend you've been standing perfectly still for hours and your neck is tired. Perfect."

Kiki glanced at Irene and said, "Is he crazy?"

Irene laughed. "Yeah, kind of."

"Sdnim ruo fo tuo era stsitra su lla," Shaun said.

"That one I *know* is nuts," Kiki said, eyeing him.

Some of the other waitresses gathered around to watch while Kiki had her portrait taken. There was a happy bohemian vibe in the room. Irene was dressed in her punked-out finery, from her ripped black high-tops to the blue skunk stripe in her hair. Shaun had found a leather Daniel Boone outfit somewhere, complete with coonskin cap, that he was sporting in style. Devon and Haley were more subdued—jeans and a peasant top for Haley, jeans and a Golden Dynasty T-shirt for Devon. He told Haley he thought he'd show the restaurant some love since Irene's usually strict father was being so nice about the photo shoot.

"Okay, Kiki, we're rolling," Haley said. She watched Kiki through the viewfinder. "What's your name?"

"Kiki Lai."

"And where are you from, Kiki?"

"I was born in Queens, but my family moved to Fort Lee when I was little. I still live there."

"How old are you?"

"Twenty-one."

"And what do you do for a living?"

"I'm a waitress here at Golden Dynasty. But I hope I'll be promoted to hostess when Irene finally goes away to college." She turned her head toward Irene and added, "You better get good grades, girl! I've been waiting a long time for this."

Irene laughed.

"Turn your head back this way," Devon said from behind his camera, where he was snapping away.

"Do you like waitressing?" Haley asked.

"Well . . . it's okay, but it's not exactly my dream job. I'm studying at night to be an accountant."

"And is that your dream job?"

"Being an accountant? No. My dream job is being a pop star. I auditioned for *American Idol* when they were in town but didn't get past the first round. I'm realistic. I know better than to hope for stardom."

"What song did you sing for your audition?" Haley asked.

Kiki burst into ". . . Baby One More Time," copying the Britney dance moves. Shaun couldn't resist joining in. Just outside the frame of the picture he wiggled his hips and sang along—"Ooh, baby baby . . ."

Devon snapped a few shots of that and then called out, "That's enough, Kiki! Back to the formal pose, please."

"Don't worry, Kiki, I've got it all right here." Haley patted her video camera.

Irene dressed the next waitress, Karen, in a gray pin-striped suit and rainbow wig. Haley interviewed her, then two waiters, then a few people Devon had brought in off the street: a tax preparer, a manicurist, a gas station attendant and a convenience store clerk, all in different, strange costumes. Irene served free shrimp toast and egg rolls and everyone seemed to enjoy themselves.

When shooting was finished, Devon, Haley, Irene and Shaun gathered at a table to wrap things up. Kiki, who was just starting the dinner shift, brought them a tray full of food, including dumplings, chicken with broccoli and shrimp lo mein.

"We shot a lot of great stuff today," Haley said.

"My favorite was that guy Kevin," Shaun said, speaking of the convenience store clerk. "Wearing that clown nose, with all that rouge on his cheeks, and his gray work shirt with 'Welcome to SpeedyShop' and 'Kevin: Munchies Maintenance Expert' on it. The expression on his face was so frickin' serious! You'd think he was the president of France or something."

"That's the genius of these portraits, Dev," Irene said. She had her laptop open and was downloading pictures from Devon's camera onto her computer to photoshop later. "They're hilarious, but touching in a way, too."

Shaun laughed. "Kevin touched my funny bone."

Suddenly Irene's face fell. "Oh my God."

"What is it?" Haley asked.

"I just clicked over to the school blog," Irene said. "Some anonymous jerk is posting unbelievable stuff about Mr. Von."

"What kind of stuff?" Devon asked.

Irene turned her laptop around so that they could see. A blogger named "the gobbler" had written:

Everybody's favorite art teacher, Mr. Rick Von, did porn in the 1970s. He was in at least 3 porno movies. I have proof.

"Oh my God," Haley said.

"This sucks!" Shaun pounded the table angrily. "This isn't true. Somebody's smearing the Von."

"Look at the comments," Irene said.

Hobitron writes: dude, show us the proof! Post it! post it online!

Trollin4chix writes: I'm kinda scared to see it. I

mean, gross. I'm curious but I'm afraid if I see mr. v
naked I'll have to claw my own eyes out.

"I'll claw Trollin4chix's eyeballs out for him,"
Shaun said.

*The gobbler replies: It's disgusting. I can't believe
this guy teaches at our school. He teaches children. He
writes grades on our art projects with the same hands
that did—that—ew, I'm gonna hurl . . . he should get
kicked out of school. If the parents knew about this
they'd totally fire him.*

Shaun's face was red with fury. "These guys just
showed their hand! This is a smear campaign. The
Vonster probably gave this gobbler dork a bad grade
in art and the kid wants revenge."

"What if it's true?" Devon asked. "The guy says
he saw Von in the movie."

"I wonder if he'd really post it," Haley said. "Or
show it to anyone."

"It's fake, I'm telling you," Shaun said. He shoved
a dumpling into his mouth, then jumped up and
paced the room. "Someone's got it in for Von. And
right before his wedding, too."

"Maybe that's what's going on," Irene said.
"Someone's trying to stop the wedding. Maybe an
old girlfriend of Mr. Von's."

"Or an old boyfriend of Mrs. Metzger's," Haley
added.

Devon shook his head. "I can't really see Dave's
mom having an old boyfriend who'd care that much."

"You never know," Irene said. "Even the geekiest people get passionate sometimes."

Haley made a face. "I really don't want to think about that while I'm eating. Or ever."

"I think someone's trying to wreck his career," Shaun said. "This blog is like a big ol' wrecking ball."

"Well, the timing's terrible for the wedding, too," Irene said. "What is Dave's mom going to say when she hears about this?"

"We'll all have to make an extra effort to be festive at the wedding," Shaun said. "To help them celebrate and forget about this filth. First line of defense: wedding clothes. Devon, can you hook me up?"

"I've got a tux with your name on it at Jack's," Devon said. "Vintage seventies polyester in mint green."

"I'm lovin' it," Shaun said.

"What about me?" Irene asked.

"We just got in this amazing gown in your size," Devon said. "I think it'd be perfect—magenta tulle with ruffles all the way down the skirt. If I had to guess, some girl wore it for her quinceañera."

"Magenta will set off your beautiful skin," Shaun said, giving Irene a big wet smack on the cheek. He was already forgetting about the crime committed against Mr. Von.

"Sounds awesome," Irene said. "Have you got anything for Haley?"

"I'll have to look around," Devon said. "But I'll find something perfect. We're getting new stuff in every day."

"Wait a minute," Irene said. "Have any of you actually been invited to the wedding?"

Devon shook his head. Shaun said, "Not officially, but I just assumed . . ."

Haley said nothing. She had received an invitation to the wedding weeks earlier. Devon, Shaun and Irene were obviously not invited. She guessed that Mr. Von wasn't inviting his students, but Dave Metzger *was* inviting his friends—and the art kids were definitely not Dave's friends.

Haley didn't want them to feel left out—and besides, she wasn't even sure if she was going to the wedding or not. She'd been invited to another wedding that day too: Sasha Lewis's father's marriage to Whitney Klein's mother. While the Metzger-Von wedding was sure to be interesting, the Lewis-Klein nuptials were the social event of the season, and Haley wasn't so certain she wanted to miss that. She couldn't go to both, but she still hadn't decided which one she'd have to turn down. So she just played along and didn't mention anything for now. Devon, Irene and Shaun would never let her hear the end of it if they knew she was even considering going to a society wedding over supporting Mr. Von in his time of need—even if they did feel left out.

● ● ●

Haley's in a tight spot. The latest news about Mr. Von is pretty shocking. Shaun's obviously convinced it's not true, but what if it is? Haley's not judgmental; it's not like her to think badly about someone just because he was once in a porn movie. If he really was. Who knows, maybe he was broke, or desperate, or did it as some kind of performance-art experiment. If he really did do it.

But she knows what Hillsdale parents are like, and their idea of progressive education does not include a porn actor teaching art to their kids. True or not, if this gets around—and how could it not?—it really could ruin Mr. Von's career.

So Haley knows she should go to Mr. Von's wedding as a show of support. It could be fun, too, if Mrs. Metzger doesn't get angry and throw the whole cake in Mr. Von's face. Even that would be a shame to miss, however sad.

But the siren song of the Lewis-Klein wedding is strong too. When Sasha's father, Jonathan Lewis, marries Whitney's mother, Linda Klein, Sasha and Whitney will become more than just friends—they'll be stepsisters. It's a big moment for them—and for three hundred of their nearest and dearest, which includes the most popular kids at school and the richest families in town. It's sure to be a blowout, and Haley's flattered to be invited.

She'd hate to miss it in favor of the depressing nuptials of an accused porn star. If that's what he is . . .

What should Haley do? If you think she should go for the glamour and attend the LEWIS-KLEIN WEDDING, turn to page 118. If you think she should stand by Mr. Von at the METZGER-VON WEDDING, turn to page 138. Finally, if you think Haley should go Switzerland on this issue and just say no to both weddings to avoid offending anyone, have her STAY HOME on page 132.

I now pronounce you
stepsisters for life.

"I, Jonathan, take thee, Linda, to be my wife. To honor and to cherish, in sickness and in health, in relapse and recovery, in the event of a life-altering disaster like a tornado or the apocalypse, wherever the four wild winds shall take us . . . I promise to accept you as you are, with all your psychological baggage, on our quest for a new and brighter lifepath together."

"Oh, God no," Cecily whispered to Haley. "They wrote their own vows."

Haley stifled a giggle. She and Cecily sat together on gold rented chairs on the perfectly manicured lawn behind the Lewis-Klein homestead. The backyard had been transformed into a garden chapel delineated by vines and flowers. Luckily, the weather was beautiful: it was a warm day in early June, the ceremony taking place in the fading light of sunset. The bride and groom stood under a canopy of green leaves dotted with white roses. Petite, perky Linda Klein—soon to be Mrs. Lewis—looked radiant in the white lace gown Whitney had designed for her, a wreath of wildflowers in her hair. And Whitney and Sasha made stunning bridesmaids.

"Whitney did a great job on the dresses, right?" Cecily whispered to Haley, and Haley agreed. Whitney and Sasha both wore long, pale blue empire-waist gowns, but with different sleeves and necklines to flatter their different figures and to keep them from looking too bridesmaidy.

Sasha's father, Jonathan Lewis, wore a gray suit with a festive pink tie and a flower in his buttonhole. He was so tall and handsome, Haley could see where Sasha had gotten her good looks. Sasha's elegant French mother, Pascale, had contributed too, of course. Mercifully, neither Pascale nor Whitney's father, Jerry, the breath spray king of New Jersey, was there to witness the remarriage of their exes.

Linda Klein was in the middle of her vow: ". . . from this day forward until the end of days, beyond death into the afterlife, should an afterlife exist, even as ghosts we will be united, though we're not saying we believe in ghosts . . ."

Haley's mind drifted as she surveyed the well-dressed crowd of wedding guests. Everybody who was anybody in Hillsdale was there. Sprinkled in among the well-to-do doctors, lawyers and business-people were their children, the most popular students at Hillsdale High School. Matt Graham and Spencer Eton, in tuxedos, sat with Coco, who wore an attention-getting shimmery silver dress, her hair in a 1920s bob. Next to Cecily was her boyfriend, football jock Drew Napolitano, and lined up beside him were Sasha's date, Johnny Lane, and Reese Highland. The three basketball teammates wore neat khaki suits and cleaned up nicely, Haley thought. Especially Reese.

The judge pronounced Linda and Jonathan husband and wife. The crowd roared its approval as the happy couple kissed passionately. Then a beaming bride and groom walked down the grassy aisle while a string quartet played and the guests threw birdseed at them. Everyone headed to the large tent set up nearby for the good part: the reception.

The swing band was already playing when Haley and her friends stepped inside the tent. "Wow," Cecily said. "This is fantastic."

The tent glowed with candles and fairy lights. There were beautifully set tables, a large dance floor and three lounge areas, with sofas and cushions surrounding low tables, for relaxing. Three bars were scattered along the sides of the tent, and a large seafood buffet was set up for appetizers.

"Holy crab claws," Drew said, diving for the buffet. "Lobster!"

There was shrimp cocktail, cold lobster, oysters and clams on the half shell. . . . It was a feast. But first, the receiving line. Haley kissed and congratulated Linda and Jonathan.

"Haley, we can't thank you enough for the beautiful video you made for us," Linda said. "It was the highlight of the rehearsal dinner."

"I'm glad you liked it," Haley said.

"I had no idea we were so alike!" Jonathan said.

"It just reaffirmed for me the fact that we're meant to be together," Linda said.

"You make a great couple," Haley said. The line was stacking up behind her, so she moved on to bridesmaids Sasha and Whitney.

"What a beautiful wedding," Haley said. "You both look gorgeous. Whitney, the dresses—"

"It's official! We're sisters!" Whitney squealed.

"I'm so happy for you both," Haley said, giving each a long hug. "Really. I wish I had a sister."

"I always wanted one too," Sasha said.

"No more only child," Whitney said. "It's going to be so great! Instead of calling all my friends in the middle of the night when I'm upset, I can just run into Sasha's room, wake her up and cry on her shoulder right then and there."

"What?" Sasha looked slightly stricken. Then she laughed. "Oh, I get it. You're kidding."

"No I'm not," Whitney said. "I'm so not kidding."

"Don't worry, Sasha," Haley said. "Just lock your bedroom door and put in some earplugs."

"Go have something to eat," Whitney said. "The caterer is amazing."

Haley accepted a lime seltzer from a passing waiter and headed for the seafood table. She dipped a shrimp in cocktail sauce.

"What did you think of the ceremony?" Reese asked. He picked up an oyster and slurped it expertly.

"Nice," Haley said. "I always love it when the bride and groom write their own vows. It makes a regular wedding ceremony seem so—so—"

"Sane?" Reese prompted with a laugh. "Seriously, is there a human being on earth capable of writing a non-lame wedding vow? I bet even Toni Morrison couldn't pull it off with a gun to her head. And she's a Nobel Prize–winner."

Haley laughed. "Can you imagine if J. D. Salinger wrote his own wedding vows? 'If you really want to hear about it, I guess I'll marry you, but I don't really feel like going into it, and I sure hope you're not a big phony. . . .'"

"Or Charles Dickens: 'I take thee in the best of times and in the worst of times—'"

"I feel like that's actually been done."

"How about the guy who wrote *Moby Dick*? 'Call me Husband.' Or how about Dr. Seuss? 'I'll marry you down on my knees, I'll marry you in purple cheese—'"

"'—I'll marry you on a star, I'll marry you in a car—'"

The two of them cracked up. Finally, Reese said, "Maybe Shakespeare could do it, but he's the only one."

"I guess it's in the nature of weddings," Haley said. "It's a sentimental occasion, so people can't help but get carried away."

"I shouldn't make fun of the ceremony," Reese said. "It really is nice to see people look so happy. Especially Whitney and Sasha. I remember what Sasha went through when her dad was losing it. It wasn't pretty. But now look at them—a brand-new family."

Haley was glad to see that Reese was in the wedding spirit. She and Whitney were the only girls in their crowd without dates to the wedding, and Haley had been hoping Reese might step up and keep her company. It was either Reese or Matt Graham, the notorious girl-izer. Haley had had a few run-ins with Matt that were less than pleasant.

The band started playing "The Summer Wind."

Reese took Haley's hand and said, "Come on, I want to get some dancing in before dinner."

Haley happily followed him to the dance floor. They tore it up while the band played a whole Frank Sinatra medley. "Gotta love Frank," Reese said. "The pride of Hoboken. You look amazing in that dress, by the way."

Haley blushed. She'd worn a deep red shift decorated with pearls at the neckline and black stiletto sandals. Her mother said that the dress brought out the russet highlights in her hair and the roses in her cheeks. For once Haley was glad she'd listened to her mother.

"I like your suit, too," she said. "We kind of match."

Reese had worn a red tie to brighten up his white shirt and khaki suit, and it was almost the exact same shade as Haley's dress. He glanced down at it and grinned. "Hey, you're right. Must have been having a mind meld with you when I got dressed this afternoon." He lifted her hand and twirled her around, dropping her into a deep dip and catching her in his arms. When the dance was over, Haley had to catch her breath—not from the effort of dancing, but from the excitement of it.

When dinner was announced, Haley was glad to see she'd been assigned the same table as Reese. They were sitting with Cecily and Drew, Coco and Spencer, Matt Graham and Johnny Lane. Whitney and Sasha sat at the head table with their parents. Sasha clanged a fork against her glass and stood up.

"I'd like to make a toast," she said. "I was a little nervous when Linda and Dad first got together. Yeah, I can admit it now." Everyone laughed lightly. "I mean, Whitney was already one of my closest friends, and I was afraid if our parents were dating it would make our friendship really weird. Like, what would happen if Linda and Dad had a fight? Would I have to hear about it? Would Whitney and I take sides?" She paused. "Actually," she added, "we do take sides: Whitney and I are both usually on Linda's side." More laughter. "Sorry, Dad. You're in a house-ful of women now, and we're all going to gang up on you!"

Jonathan raised his hands in surrender and said, "I give up already!"

"But really, it's turned out to be more wonderful than I ever imagined," Sasha said. "I have a great new stepmom and a great new stepsister, and I couldn't be happier. Here's to Linda and Dad!"

Everyone clinked glasses and clapped, and then Whitney stood up to make her toast. Haley braced herself for awkwardness: Whitney wasn't as graceful a speaker as Sasha.

"Thanks, Sasha. You're the greatest stepsister ever—I just wish we were the same size so we could share clothes! Seriously, the diet starts tomorrow. I just want to say that I wish Mom and Jon all the best and many happy reruns. Welcome to the family, Jon and Sasha!"

"That was sweet," Cecily said.

"'Many happy reruns'?" Coco shook her head. "Leave it to Whitney to screw up her mom's wedding toast."

"Leave her alone, Coco," Reese said. "We all know what she meant."

"Besides, it was kind of cute," Haley said. "It was so Whitney."

More clinking, more drinking, more applause, and dinner began. Every so often someone tapped a glass and Jon and Linda had to stop whatever they were doing and kiss.

"Did you know Mr. Von is getting married tonight too?" Johnny Lane said. "I wonder what's happening at *that* wedding."

Haley felt a twinge of guilt. She'd been invited to Mr. Von's wedding but had decided to come to this one instead. Not that she regretted it. There was no way Mr. Von's wedding was as fabulous as this one.

"Don't you mean Mr. Perv?" Coco said. "Have you seen those rumors about him on the Web?"

"What rumors?" Cecily asked.

"Somebody wrote an anonymous post saying they have proof that Mr. Von used to be in porn movies," Drew said. "I guess they've seen the films. I say, post 'em if you got 'em."

"But who would do that?" Reese said. "That could ruin his teaching career."

"You're not kidding," Coco said. "I think he should be fired and hounded out of town."

"But it's just a rumor, Coco," Haley said. "You don't know for sure if it's true."

"Yeah, somebody could be out to get him for some reason," Johnny said.

"What's this dude like?" Matt Graham asked. He was a boarding-school friend of Spencer's but they'd both been kicked out. Now Spencer went to Hillsdale and Matt went to Ridgewood, a rival school.

"Actually, I can totally picture him as a seventies porn star," Johnny said. "He's tall and thin and rumpled, and he's usually got about three days' worth of stubble on his chin—"

"—and he talks in this deep, raspy voice," Spencer said, lowering his voice in a bad imitation of Mr. Von. "Come here, little girl, want to see my magic pencil?"

Coco slapped his arm and said, "Is that any way for the governor's son to talk?"

Everybody cracked up. Spencer, whose mother had just been elected governor, almost never acted in a politically correct way. In fact, his own mother had sent him away for the winter break in an attempt to keep him out of trouble and out of the paparazzi's sights. It didn't work, of course; Spencer was an expert at finding trouble wherever he went.

"I can't believe it's true," Cecily said.

"You never know what people have done in their former lives," Drew said. "Teachers can be especially weird in private. That's what I've heard, anyway."

"Yeah, that's what you heard on late-night cable," Johnny said.

"Do you think they went through with the wedding?" Haley said. "Maybe Mrs. Metzger called it off when she heard the rumors."

"My sources never said it was canceled," Coco said. "But I heard that, like, half the guests who RSVP'd weren't planning to show up. Not that I condone that sort of rudeness, but I don't blame them. The man's a pariah now. Who'd want to be associated with him?"

Haley felt terrible. Had half the guests really not shown up? Poor Mr. Von, and poor Mrs. Metzger.

"Aw, come on," Drew said. "So the guy was in a porn movie thirty years ago. What's so bad about that?"

"What's so bad about it, Drew," Coco snapped, "besides the moral and public health issues and the utter grossness of the whole thing, is the reputation of our school. What will colleges think when we apply next year and they see that we come from the school that hires porn actors as teachers?"

"I think that's a little extreme, Coco," Reese said.

"Spencer, I think you should make your mother

form a task force or something, and get the school board to fire Mr. Von," Coco said.

Spencer forked a bit of salmon into his mouth. "Sure thing, Coco. I'll get right on that. It's not like she has anything important to do, like run the state of New Jersey."

"I'd feel bad if their wedding didn't go well tonight," Haley said. "It's times like this that they need the support of their friends more than ever. I wonder what Dave thinks about the scandal?"

"Hearing his new stepdad is a porn star?" Johnny said. "That dork probably went catatonic."

"Either that, or he'll hit up Mr. V for tips on how to handle chicks," Drew said. Cecily gave him a disapproving slap on the hand.

"You boys are so filthy-minded," she said. "I want to know, who's spreading all these nasty rumors in the first place?"

"So do I," Haley said. "What has that person got to gain from all this?"

"Can we talk about something else?" Matt said. "Not to dis your school or anything, but I don't know the dude, and I really don't care. Besides, I'm trying to eat."

The conversation switched to sports while the plates were cleared, and then the band returned to the stage. Reese tapped Haley's arm gently.

"Come on, dance partner. I'm going to slip the

bandleader a twenty and request all Sinatra, all night long. We've got some dancing to do."

Haley smiled and happily danced the night away with Reese. There was cake, there were more toasts, there were tossed bouquets and garters and jokes, but Haley liked dancing with Reese best of all. Late that night when the band finally packed up their instruments, the two of them were still slow-dancing among the twinkling lights, exhausted but happy, to "One for My Baby." Reese had it on his iPod, and they shared the earbuds, one in Haley's ear and one in Reese's.

"We can't move too far apart or the earbuds will pop out," Reese whispered. "So you better stay close."

She did.

● ● ●

For Haley, the Lewis-Klein union was just what a wedding should be: an affair to remember. Reese was on his most charming and gentlemanly behavior, dancing the night away with Haley. Good food, good music, great people and even some gossip—this wedding had it all. Haley will remember that night for the rest of her life. How do you top an evening like that?

Maybe you don't—not for a while, anyway. Time for Haley to return to earth and focus on some upcoming issues in her life. Issue number one: the prom. Who will she go with? What will she wear?

Issue number two: her schoolwork. Where does she stand in the class rankings? Has the recent effort she's put into studying paid off?

Issue number three: what's behind the Mr. Von rumors? Are they really true? And how will this affect him at school?

If you think Haley's fired up to make plans for the prom, go to page 145, GAGGLE OF GIRLS. If you think she's more curious about her grades, go to page 152, CHECK GRADES. If you think she needs to catch up on the latest school scandal, go to page 156, PRINCIPAL CRUM'S LITANY.

STAY HOME

Sometimes the best decision is
no decision at all.

"Honey, why aren't you dressed?"

Haley's parents paused by the door of her room, peering in at her. She was lying on her bed in sweats reading *Pride and Prejudice*.

"I thought you were going to the Lewis-Klein wedding tonight," Joan said.

"No," Perry said. "I thought she was going to Mr. Von's wedding."

"I'm not going to either one," Haley said. "I

called Whitney and Dave and told them both I was too sick to go out. I just couldn't face it."

Haley had been torn between her two sets of friends. The wedding between Sasha's father and Whitney's mother was one of the biggest days of their lives—turning the two friends into sisters—and one of the biggest events in town. Haley knew they'd be crushed if they heard she had turned down their invitation to go to the Metzger-Von wedding instead. They might even get so angry with her they wouldn't speak to her.

But for Dave Metzger, his mother's wedding was a milestone too. Not only was it traumatic for him to be gaining a new father—especially one who taught at his school—he was still recovering from the rejection by his biological father. And then there were the rumors circulating about Mr. Von—some anonymous blogger claimed to have actual film of Mr. Von acting in a porno movie. That had to be even more agonizing for Dave. Haley could hear his whining now: his mom was marrying a porn star! So the Metzger-Von clan was in crisis, and Haley knew they could use her support. If Dave and his friends heard that she'd gone to the more glamorous and fun Lewis-Klein wedding instead, they'd feel betrayed.

She wished she could go to both weddings, but it was physically impossible. As Haley saw it, her only choice was to go to neither.

"I understand, sweetie," Joan said. "You had a tough decision to make."

"I just didn't want to hurt anyone's feelings," Haley said.

"Well, I for one am thrilled to have you home with us on a Saturday night," Perry said. "And I think I know someone else who'll be glad to have you around."

"Mitchell." She didn't spend enough time with her little brother, and she felt guilty about it. She knew he was lonely and needed his sister. In a year she'd be leaving for college and he'd be home by himself all the time, a virtual only child.

"Let's have a movie night tonight," Joan said. "I'll make popcorn and we can watch whatever you and Mitchie want."

Haley smiled. "Sounds awesome."

After dinner, the whole family gathered around the wide-screen monitor in the living room. Haley couldn't remember the last time they'd all spent an evening together like this. Mitchell seemed almost in shock.

"What time are you leaving, Haley?" he asked.

"I'm not," she replied. "I'm staying in tonight."

"No, but really," Mitchell said. "When are you going out?"

"Mitchell, I'm not going anywhere."

"I heard you. But how long till you have to go meet your friends?"

Haley sighed and shook her head. Mitchell could be a little weird. She really should spend more time with him. "Mitchell, I'm all about school now. No more socializing. From now until the end of the year, I'm a grind."

Her father glanced at her in surprise. "Really? Since when?"

Haley shrugged. "Since spring break, I guess. I've really gotten into my AP History class. I just want to see how far I can go if I study really hard."

Her mother said, "We'll see how long that lasts."

"How did you do on your history test last week?" Perry asked.

"I don't know," Haley said. "I think I did okay, but we find out on Monday."

Mitchell said, "Haley, I just want to know what time you are going out."

She pretended to look at a watch on her wrist. It was Saturday night; she had no plans to go anywhere until it was time for school on Monday morning. "Mitchell, I'm leaving in thirty-six hours. Does that satisfy you?"

He nodded soberly. "Yes. Thank you for giving me fair warning."

"Mitchell gets to pick the first movie tonight," Perry said. "What'll it be, my boy?"

"*WALL-E,*" Mitchell declared.

They snuggled together on the couch, all four of them, and munched popcorn while watching

WALL-E. Haley got to pick the second movie. It was past Mitchell's bedtime, but their parents had decided to let him stay up late just this once, so Haley chose something she knew Mitchell would like: *Coraline*. The movie where the seemingly perfect parents who live on the other side of the wall turn out to be not so perfect after all.

The movie was scary, but of the four Millers, Mitchell seemed the least bothered by it. "Mom, if you have any buttons you don't need, will you give them to me?" he said. "I want to make a face like that with button eyes."

"Do you mean, like a doll?" Joan asked. "Or a mask, on a paper plate?"

"Sure, yes," Mitchell said, entranced by the movie. "On a paper plate. That would work."

Haley shuddered but told herself he was only being creative.

Later that night Haley got a text from Irene. "Come over 2 my house after school monday—must talk. Big news."

Haley texted back, "What big news? Tell me."

Irene wrote back, "Just come over."

● ● ●

Haley may have missed two weddings, but at least she avoided hurting anyone's feelings. On Monday morning she can go back to school without worrying about having made any enemies. So that's something.

Of course, she is probably curious about what she missed at both weddings. But Irene's text is especially intriguing. What is her big news? Had she heard some gossip about one of the weddings? Something about the Mr. Von rumors? Or is the news on a completely different topic, like, say, Devon McKnight? Why couldn't she just text it to Haley, or call her? Should Haley care?

Now you must help her make her next move. If you think Haley was serious when she announced her intention to become a study-holic and that grind is the new black, have her check on her academic status on page 152, CHECK GRADES. If you think she's dying to know what Irene's big news is, go to page 162, IN CONFIDENCE. If you think she should get the latest update on the Mr. Von scandal and anything else happening at school, go to page 156, PRINCIPAL CRUM'S LITANY.

METZGER-VON WEDDING

Any wedding can be fun if you have the right attitude.

"Hey—there's no place card here for RoBro!" Dave said. He was scanning the table that held the place cards for every wedding guest—the name of the guest and which table they were assigned to—but there was no card that said *RoBro!* Understandably, Haley thought, but obviously she said nothing to Dave.

Dave started to sweat in that panicky way he had. "Mom!" he shouted. "Mom!" Nora Metzger—now Mrs. Nora Von—came running over to her son.

"What is it, darling?" She pulled him to her in an emotional hug. He pushed away.

"Which table is RoBro! sitting at?" he demanded. "I don't see his name here."

"He's sitting at table one with us, of course," Nora said. "Here's his place card." She pulled out a card with *ROB* written on it in calligraphy. "I guess the calligrapher misread the name."

"Whew. Oh. Okay." Dave began to calm down. Haley exchanged a glance with Annie, Dave's girl-friend. Crisis averted. They both had a fair amount of experience with Dave and his crises.

Dave picked up his robot brother and carried him to table 1, where he sat the robot down in front of his own place setting. Haley realized RoBro! was sort of like a security blanket for Dave, or a metal teddy bear. And Dave was like a needy six-year-old who could hardly go anywhere without it.

"I hope for his sake he grows out of this before college," Annie whispered to Haley.

"I'm right with you," Haley said.

The seating of RoBro! was only one odd moment at a deeply odd wedding. The ceremony itself took place under a tree in Mr. Von's backyard. Mr. Von and Mrs. Metzger were married by an aging hippie dressed like a jester who claimed to be a minister of the Church of the Merry Prankster. The small group of guests—apparently only about half the invited guests had shown up, maybe thirty or forty people,

Haley guessed, and a lot of empty seats—stood and watched while Rick Von promised to dig on the grooviness of his bride, Nora Metzger, and Nora vowed not to impede her husband Rick's creative energy. To seal their vow they danced some kind of medieval jig and then kissed. Haley kept an eye on Dave the whole time. His feud with Annie, whatever it had been about, seemed to be over, at least on his side. He gripped Annie's hand throughout the ceremony until her fingers went white.

Everyone then trooped across the weedy lawn to the patchwork tent Mr. Von had made himself from swatches of fabric from various times of his life: bits of clothes and bedspreads and curtains and other things that had meaning for him. The last of the day's sunlight poured in through the multicolored fabric, giving the tent a rainbow glow. It was a funky place for a wedding reception—very much an artist's vision—but Haley admired all the personal and original touches.

Haley strolled past a knot of Hillsdale teachers on her way to the drinks table. She recognized Mr. Lyons, the drama teacher, Ms. Storch, who taught English, and a few others. They were looking around furtively and whispering.

"I count at least five teachers who didn't show," Ms. Storch said. "Ruth told me last week she was coming— where is she? And Marianne's not here, and Clay—"

"People are nervous," Mr. Lyons said. "No one wants to be associated with such a touchy issue."

"I say now's the time to stand up for him, not hide," another woman said. "We shouldn't be such cowards."

"It's the fear," Mr. Lyons said. "The parents and the school board go crazy over nothing. Something like this can ruin everybody associated with it. We should all hope we're not accused of participating in an orgy just by being at his wedding. I'm serious. A witch hunt can happen like *that*." He snapped his fingers dramatically.

Haley knew they must be talking about the rumors about Mr. Von, which had spread like poison ivy over the Internet. Someone had posted a blog entry on the school site accusing Mr. Von of having been in porn movies in the seventies. The accuser claimed to have proof—actual footage. Nobody else had seen this footage yet, and Mr. Von's defenders tried to brush off the accusations by saying it must be someone out to get him. Mr. Von himself had completely ignored the rumors. Haley wondered if he even knew about them. But he couldn't be that out of it, could he?

Ms. Storch caught sight of Haley hovering nearby and nudged Mr. Lyons to make him shut up. Haley nodded and smiled at them as if she hadn't overheard. "Hi! Nice wedding, huh?"

The teachers all plastered smiles on their faces and chorused, "Very nice. Very touching." Haley moved on to the drinks table as fast as she could.

Annie was already there with Hannah Moss and Alex Martin, ordering lime rickeys. "Have you heard the way some of these people are talking?" Annie said. "Why did they come to the wedding if they're just going to spend the whole evening gossiping about the groom? Seems awfully rude to me."

A cater-waiter walked by with a tray of chicken-liver spread over crackers. He offered some to Haley and her friends.

"No thanks," Haley said.

"No thanks," Annie sniffed.

"Definitely no thanks," Hannah said.

"I'll have one." Alex took a cracker and ate it. "Not bad."

"How's Dave handling the rumors?" Haley asked Annie.

"Surprisingly well," Annie said. "It's like he's blocking it out or something. Every once in a while he'll mutter something under his breath like, 'I knew it. I knew it.' But that's not so unusual . . . for him."

The three-piece band—guitar, fiddle and stand-up bass—set up near the small dance floor. "Hey there, everybody, we're a jazz-bluegrass-fusion combo called the Blues-berries, and we're here to get your feet moving."

The music started, and Alex caught Haley's eye. "You know what? We're at a wedding. We're here to have a good time. Haley, would you like to dance?"

"I'd love to." They joined Mr. and Mrs. Von on the dance floor. Jazz-bluegrass fusion turned out to be not the easiest music to dance to, but Alex and

Haley made do by creating their own blend of square dancing, waltzing and pogoing.

The dinner itself was kind of strange, what with the choice of entrees being lamb shank or tofu steak, with beet and radish puree to start. Dave tried to feed RoBro! salad, which dribbled down his metal front.

"I think I could have predicted that," Alex whispered to Haley, who laughed quietly.

Mr. Von stood to toast his new bride by calling her "the sexiest woman I've ever met," which caused a few titters among the guests and made Dave bite his lip so hard it bled. They danced their first dance to the first track on John Coltrane's *A Love Supreme*—a beautiful jazz tune but very long—oblivious to the whispers and gossip all around them at their own wedding.

In spite of the strangeness, Haley had a good time, mostly because of Alex. He was the only one who seemed to see the wedding the way Haley saw it, from a slight distance, one step away. It was strange and touching, beautiful in its own way, but funny, too. Haley didn't want to be disrespectful, but the funny little comments she and Alex made to each other during the reception made the whole ordeal a lot more fun.

"Dave's staying at my house while his parents are away on their honeymoon," Annie told Haley as she was getting ready to go home. "You should come over and visit."

"Where are they going on their honeymoon?" Haley asked.

"Hawaii. They rented a grass hut on the beach. Isn't that romantic?"

"Very."

Alex gave her a kiss on the cheek as she left. She couldn't tell what kind of kiss he'd meant it to be, a friendly peck or more. As she drove home, she wondered what she'd missed at Sasha and Whitney's big bash. Still, she was glad she'd gone to the Vons' wedding. They needed all the friends they could get.

● ● ●

If Haley was looking for material to fuel her art, the Vons' wedding should provide her with enough strange imagery to last a lifetime. Every time she steps into the world of Dave Metzger, she feels as if she's gone through the looking glass to crazyland. And she always finds herself drawn to the one other sane person in that nutty circle: Alex. Being two sensible people in a world of crackpots gives them a kind of bond.

Now that the wedding is over, Haley's ready to move on. If you think she wants to go back to hitting the books hard, send her to CHECK GRADES on page 152. If you think she'd like to know more about the latest rumors circulating at school, go to page 156, PRINCIPAL CRUM'S LITANY. If you think she ought to go over to Annie's house to check up on Dave's mental state, go to page 168, DADDY DEAREST.

Nothing inspires social engineering like prom night.

"Let's get down to business," Coco said. She stirred artificial sweetener into her half-caf skim latte. "We all know we're not really here to rehash Whitney and Sasha's fabulous wedding for the hundredth time." She flashed her teeth at Whitney in a sickening smile. "It was lovely, but that's the past. The next big event in our lives is the prom."

Everyone at the table nodded. When Coco had demanded that Whitney, Sasha, Cecily and Haley meet her at Drip for an after-school coffee, Haley had a feeling the prom was going to come up.

"Coco, the fabric for your dress is coming in today," Whitney said with a nervous false brightness. "So don't worry, the dress will be ready in plenty of time. I know you're going to love it."

"I'd better love it, or you won't be having much fun at the prom," Coco said. "But we'll get to dresses later. First things first: dates."

Haley shifted in her seat. She didn't have a prom date yet. In fact, her whole prom situation was wide open. Anything was possible, from going alone, to going with Reese Highland, to going with some geek she could barely stomach. But it didn't matter what Haley wanted—Coco seemed to have something in mind for her already.

"Some of us have boyfriends, so our prom dates are all set," Coco said. "We all know who I'm talking about—Cecily's going with Drew, I'm going with Spencer, and Sasha, I'm assuming you're going with Johnny, right? Or is that still just a casual hookup situation?"

"No, we're totally back together," Sasha said. "He's already got a new leather jacket to wear that night."

Coco wrinkled her nose. "How rock of him. Sasha, I have to say your taste was always in the gutter. Moving on—"

"Just because he's not some uptight short-haired

preppy mama's boy with too much money and too many DWIs doesn't mean he's not hot," Sasha shot back.

Coco brushed this off. "I said, moving on . . . That leaves our two problem children, Whitney and Haley."

Haley squirmed under the sudden intense scrutiny of Coco, Sasha and Cecily. She glanced at Whitney. "Do you feel like a paramecium under a microscope right now? Because I do."

"I don't know what a paramedicum is, but if it feels bad when it's under a microscope, then yes," Whitney replied.

"No need to worry, single girls," Coco said. "I've got it all figured out. You will both have the perfect dates, and you will both have the time of your lives."

"What do you mean, you have it all figured out?" Haley said. "No one's asked me to the prom yet."

"You don't have to wait to be asked, Haley," Coco said. "I'm pulling the strings behind the scenes. All you have to do is go along for the ride. Isn't that nice and easy? I wish somebody would run my life for me so I wouldn't have to do everything for myself all the time. You should consider yourself lucky."

Haley did not like the sound of this at all. Whenever Coco "pulled the strings behind the scenes," the biggest beneficiary usually turned out to be Coco herself. Haley braced for the worst.

"Each of us will be asked to the prom officially, in

style," Coco said. "I'll make sure the boys do their part to make this the most romantic prom night of our lives. You won't be disappointed."

Whitney's left knee was jiggling up and down in excitement. "Okay, but who's my date going to be?"

"Whitney, this year you're going to the prom with . . ." Coco paused for drama. "Reese Highland."

"What?" Whitney squealed with delight. "Are you kidding me? Oh my God!"

Haley felt as if she'd been punched in the stomach. Reese with Whitney? That didn't make sense. So who was left for Haley?

Coco turned her laser eyes to her. "And Haley, your date will be Matt Graham."

Another punch to the gut. Matt Graham, the skeeviest skeeve in town? He was supposed to be Haley's prom date?

"But he doesn't even go to our school," Haley protested. "How can he ask me when it's not even his prom?"

"That's a technicality," Coco said. "The point is, he has to go with one of us or he won't be able to go at all. And how can we let Matt miss such a big night out with all his friends? So you're up. Take one for the team, Haley."

Whitney laid a sympathetic hand on Haley's arm. "It won't be so bad, Haley. Matt's really cute."

"He's an octopus," Haley complained. "Mr.

Hands." Matt had a terrible reputation as a love-'em-and-leave-'em makeout artist who couldn't keep his hands to himself. Haley had had several run-ins with him before, and they'd never ended pleasantly. He was certainly cute, and Haley had always suspected Whitney of having a crush on him.

"Why can't I go with Reese?" she asked. "And Whitney with Matt, if she thinks he's so cute?"

Coco shook her head firmly. "Whitney is going with Reese. Period. I'm sorry, Haley, but it's better for everyone if you and Reese don't go together. You know your history with him."

"My history?"

"The fights, the breakups, the misunderstandings, the getting back together," Cecily said. "I know you like him, Haley, but you have to admit it's been a rocky road."

"And you and Reese are the only couple that hasn't gotten back together since the great mass breakup last winter," Sasha added. "Don't you think that says something?"

Okay, so her relationship with Reese had been something of a roller coaster. Whose relationship wasn't? Coco and Spencer had broken up and gotten together more times than she could count. So had Sasha and Johnny.

"That doesn't mean we shouldn't go to the prom together," Haley said. "Reese and Whitney—no of-fense, Whit, but that just feels weird to me."

Coco patted her knee condescendingly. "You'll get used to the idea. It has to be this way, Haley. Trust me. This way there's no possibility of you and Reese causing some major drama that ruins the evening for everyone."

Fuming, Haley bit her lip to keep herself from saying something she'd regret. Coco had reverted to her most manipulative, aggressive queen-bee self, and Haley was feeling the pain of her sting firsthand.

● ● ●

Ouch—low blow from Coco. Whitney and Reese at the prom together? How will Haley be able to stomach that? It's just wrong in so many ways.

What is Coco thinking? Is she getting revenge on Haley for some transgression Haley doesn't remember committing? Is she just being mean for the fun of it? Is she reveling in her power to manipulate the Hillsdale social scene any way she likes, no matter how twisted?

Haley has to tread carefully here. Coco will not be crossed, and she hates it when she doesn't get her way. Basically, Haley has three choices: she can go along for the ride and see where it takes her; she can fight the power, refuse to go along with Coco's machinations and take matters into her own hands; or she can opt out, step aside and refuse to play Coco's game altogether.

If you think Haley is helpless against Coco and should simply accept her fate and go to the prom with Matt Graham, go to SINGING TELEGRAM on page 178.

If you think Haley should be assertive and ask Reese to the prom herself—screw Coco and her little plans—go to page 186, ASK REESE. If you think Haley should tell Coco to leave her out of her little schemes and take her chances on going to the prom with whoever happens to ask her, go to PORCH-SWING PROPOSAL on page 189.

Coco can try to manipulate the prom however she wants. That's not to say everything has to go according to plan.

Smart girls have more fun.

"**H**ow did you do?"

Reese materialized next to Haley in the hall outside Mr. Tygert's AP History classroom. Haley had been so absorbed in looking for her name on the list posted on the door that she hadn't heard him coming.

"Not sure yet—I just got here," she said, smiling nervously.

The previous week, Haley had taken the biggest AP History test of the semester, and she was anxious

PRINCIPAL CRUM'S LITANY

Something is rotten in the state of New Jersey.

"The halls of this school are rank with a foul stench."

Principal Crum began his speech to the schoolwide assembly he'd called—Code Carnelian—with his usual grace and poetry. Haley slipped into a seat by the auditorium door and buckled up for the usual wild ride on the Crum-coaster. In Principal Crum's eyes something always seemed to be rotten in the state of Hillsdale; it was just a matter of which particular student calamity was causing the stink this time.

to find out her grade. Mr. Tygert had announced that he would post the grades that morning, so Haley got to school earlier than usual to check. She'd been studying so hard lately, especially for history, that she'd be very disappointed if she didn't get a good grade.

Always the gentleman, Reese stepped aside and let her check her grade in peace. "Ladies first."

"Thanks." Haley ran her finger down the list of names until she got to *Miller, Haley—97=A.*

"Yes!" she said quietly to herself. She tried not to look too triumphant as she told the waiting Reese, "I got an A."

"Congratulations!" Reese scanned the list for his name, then held his hand up for Haley to give him five. "Me too! Ninety-five!"

"Awesome!" Haley slapped his hand, secretly glad she'd gotten a slightly higher score than he did, and also relieved he'd done well enough that she wouldn't have to feel awkward about it.

"I knew you'd ace the test," Reese said. "You've been on fire in class lately."

"Thanks," Haley said. "I knew you'd ace it because you always ace everything."

"That's not true," Reese said modestly, but it pretty much was. "Listen, Haley—there's something I need to ask you. Would it be okay if I stopped by your house on Sunday afternoon to talk for a minute?"

Talk? What could Reese possibly want to talk about? And who was Haley to say no? She hesitated just a moment, wanting to be sure she'd be home that afternoon. Her mother had said something about wanting her to take Mitchell to a birthday party, but was it Saturday or Sunday . . . ?

Before she had a chance to reply, Alex Martin bounded up to them, excited to see the list. "Everybody happy?" he asked, scanning their faces for joy or misery. "Looks that way. Let's see how my favorite protégée did." He read the list, stopping at Reese's A first—"Way to go, Reese"—and then Haley's.

"Highest grade in the class," Alex said, beaming at her. "Not too shabby."

"Thanks," Haley said.

Reese shifted from one foot to the other, looking uncomfortable. "Um, listen," he said to Haley, "let me know about Sunday when you have a chance, okay?"

"I will," she promised. He walked away. It was strange to see Reese, the gracious prince of the junior class, acting so awkward. What was going on with him? Haley wondered. What did he want to ask her about that required making an appointment with her first?

Once he was out of sight, Alex said, "Great job on that test—I knew you could do it."

"Thanks," she said again. The first-period bell rang.

"I've got to run," Alex said. [...] thing I really need to talk to you a[...] your house later?"

● ● ●

Hmmm. Two boys, each asking the sa[...] which is, Can I ask you a question? Late[...] What could that question be? Haley doesn[...] sure, but she suspects it may have something [...] the prom.

If she's right, and if she wants to avoid the aw[...] ness of having to say no to a boy she likes—and sh[...] them both, if not equally—she needs to decide [...] she'd like to see ringing her doorbell this weekend. O[...] she'd rather take matters into her own hands and a[...] someone to the prom herself. Why wait to be asked? That's so prefeminist.

If you think Haley is most curious to know what Reese wants to ask her, go to page 189, PORCH-SWING PROPOSAL. If you think Alex's question might be more interesting, go to page 194, THE TRADITIONALIST. If you think Haley likes Reese the best and knows it, and should stop waiting around and playing games and just ask him to the prom already, go to page 186, ASK REESE.

"And that stench is called gossip," Principal Crum continued. "The rumor mill. The anonymous scourge of the Internet. Someone has started false gossip about one of our esteemed teachers here at Hillsdale High. That gossip is affecting this teacher's career, the reputation of the school and the lives of you, the students—each and every one of you!"

Haley heard giggling behind her and turned to see Coco De Clerq and her coterie—Sasha Lewis, Cecily Watson and Whitney Klein—giggling while flashing through photos on Coco's cell phone. Probably candid shots from the wedding of Whitney's mother to Sasha's father. The terrible scourge of the school could be poison fire ants crawling from the ceiling and they wouldn't notice. Their default response to Principal Crum was to tune him out.

"Someone—a student in this very school—has written terrible things about this teacher on the school Web site. I won't say which teacher it is, to protect his privacy, or what's left of it. I'd hate to see the art room bombarded with jokey hate graffiti or whatever you spawn of Satan like to do in your free time. Wait—oops. I shouldn't have said 'the art room.' I meant his classroom, any old classroom in the building, not the art room per se."

Haley glanced back to the very last row, where she knew she'd find the arty crowd—Devon McKnight, Irene Chen and Shaun Willkommen—hiding out. Devon and Irene were doodling in their notebooks while they listened to the principal's rant, but Shaun sat ramrod straight, outraged at the smearing of his favorite teacher. Unless Shaun was a better actor than he seemed, he was definitely not the perpetrator, Haley decided.

"Just a few examples of the heinous lies this good-for-nothing is spreading about a respected teacher," Principal Crum said, pausing to read from some blog copy he'd printed out. "'Mr. Von is a porno-pervert.'" The blood drained from Principal Crum's face as he realized he'd slipped up again. "I don't mean Mr. Von. I mean any teacher *like* Mr. Von. It could be anyone. To continue: 'I've seen him on film naked with young women. They're talking and using words like "seminal." He shouldn't be allowed to even breathe the same air as the kids in this town.'"

Snickers from a group of jocks to Haley's right— Drew Napolitano, Spencer Eton, Johnny Lane and Reese Highland. Could any of them have done this? Haley wondered. She didn't see why they would. What would they have against Mr. Von?

"First of all, this kind of vile language is not tolerated on the school Web site," Principal Crum said. "But more importantly, the person writing these words and all the anonymous commenters like 'spellsliketeenspirit' and 'groinkicker' are cowards. They think they're brave making these bold statements about a teacher, but they're too chicken to sign their own accusations. This is a grave matter, people—a matter of character! Moral fiber! Stand up and show us what you're made of! Do you children want to grow up to be moral sissies with no fiber whatsoever?"

Up ahead, in the first row, sat the brain trust: Alex Martin, Hannah Moss, Annie Armstrong and Dave Metzger. Mr. Von had just married Dave's mother. What was Dave's reaction to these embarrassing rumors? Was there any chance he thought they were true?

It was hard to tell just by watching Dave. He did look upset, but then, he was a neurotic person and it was unusual to see him not looking upset.

"This makes me sad," Principal Crum said insincerely. "Juniors and seniors, your prom is coming up. I feel sorry for you, that you will have to attend this milestone in your young lives in such a fetid atmosphere of mistrust and filth. Very sorry for you. I believe the only thing that can save your prom from utter failure is the cleanliness of confession. If the anonymous accuser comes clean, your prom will be purified and saved from the sleaze!"

Haley was confused: what did the Mr. Von scandal have to do with the prom? But then, she often was confused during Principal Crum's endless, incoherent rants.

"Whoever you are, anonymous accuser, I command

you to stand up right here and now and make yourself known!"

Principal Crum paused to see if anyone took the bait. Predictably, no one did. The auditorium was still except for a few awkward coughs.

"I thought so. You are a coward. Well, never fear, anonymous coward. We will find you. We will smoke you out before you have a chance to publish more salacious rumors and you will be severely punished. Severely. Punished."

He paused again for effect. Someone yawned. As far as Haley could tell, he'd threatened to punish someone so many times that no one really cared anymore.

"That is all for now. You are dismissed."

● ● ●

Principal Crum is on the rampage again, and not very good at keeping the victim's identity a secret. Poor Mr. Von; if anyone didn't know he was the target of pornography accusations before, they know now. Haley would like to put this scandal behind her and focus on the filthy, sleazy prom coming up. She doesn't have a date yet and there are a lot of choices. She may not get to choose exactly who her date will be, but she can decide which crowd she wants to run with on prom night.

So, if you think Haley would like to have a glamorous prom night with the ritzy Coco crowd, turn to page 178, SINGING TELEGRAM. If you think she's more in the mood for a funky time with Devon and the artistes, go to page 191, HOLY ROLLER RECORDS. If you think her recent excellent grades in AP History have her leaning toward Alex and the brain trust, go to page 194, THE TRADITIONALIST. If you think Haley knows for sure who she wants to go to the prom with, and it's Reese and only Reese, have her ASK REESE on page 186. Finally, if you think she should just hang back and see what comes her way, turn to page 189, PORCH-SWING PROPOSAL.

IN CONFIDENCE

Coco De Clerq is not the only schemer in school.

"**W**hat's the big news?" Haley arrived at Irene's house dying to know why she had to show up in person to hear the secret Irene was keeping. "Why couldn't you just text me?"

"First, because it's complicated," Irene said. "And second, because I wanted to talk to you without Shaun around, and Shaun's always around. In fact, he's coming over in half an hour so we better get to it. But first—again—the hostess in me cannot allow you into my house without offering you something to eat or drink. Want something? We've got tea, soda and cold spare ribs in the fridge."

"No thanks," Haley said, impatient. "Just tell me what's up."

"Okay." Irene settled down at the kitchen table. "The other night Devon and I were over at Shaun's, and the prom came up. Shaun brought it up, actually, because he's obsessively planning who he wants to be for prom and can't make up his mind. Right now it's between Bigfoot and some kind of space alien. I keep telling him it's not Halloween, it's the prom, but trying to get through his thick skull is like—"

"Okay, okay," Haley said. "But what does this have to do with me?"

The kettle whistled and Irene got up to make tea. "Sure you don't want some? We've got ginger-mint."

"Yes, okay, whatever. Just tell me!"

"So anyway, Devon let it slip that he hasn't asked anyone to the prom yet, but he definitely wants to go. So I asked him who he'd ask if he could ask anyone, and he refused to say. We bugged him and bugged him until finally Shaun had him pinned on the floor with some kind of wrestling death grip and forced it out of him."

"And—?"

"You," Irene said with satisfaction. "If he could ask anyone to the prom it would be you."

Haley's heart pounded. This was exciting news. "So why doesn't he ask me?"

"Because he's afraid you'll say no," Irene said. "You know Devon, always has to be Mr. Cool. So scared of looking like an idiot that sometimes he gets kind of passive."

Haley totally knew what Irene was talking about. It had been the main obstacle between her and Devon ever getting together. Well, that, and the machinations of one conniving bleached-blond freshman named Darcy Podowski.

And that was the problem: Haley liked Devon a lot. But sometimes she wanted someone who was willing to go out on a limb and declare that he really wanted *her* and only her. She often wondered if Devon would be present enough for her. Of course, there was one way to find out: give him a shot.

"So?" Irene said. "If he asked you, what would you say?"

"I'm not sure," Haley said.

Irene rolled her eyes. "You two. I had a feeling you'd say that. That's where my brilliant plan comes in. It makes the whole situation a lot more complicated, but it seems to me you and Devon like things that way."

"What's the plan?"

"Basically, you have twenty-four hours to think about who you want to go to the prom with, and if you decide you want to go with Devon, meet him at Holy Roller Records at three p.m. tomorrow. He'll be there waiting for you, and he knows that's the signal that it's safe for him to put himself out and actually let a girl know he likes her. Meaning you."

"Sounds like a plan."

"But don't be late, and don't be wishy-washy or you'll screw the whole thing up," Irene warned. "Devon has a face-saving backup plan. That's where the complications come in."

"Let me guess—Darcy."

"Correct. If you turn him down, Darcy's his backup date. But the Troll already asked Darcy, so Devon doesn't have much time to snag her. She put off the Troll for a few days because she wants to see if Devon will ask her. But the Troll won't wait forever. And if Devon asks you, she'll go with him."

"She'd really go to the prom with the Troll?" Garrett "the Troll" Noll was a greasy-haired skater dude from the Floods. He and his best friend, Chopper, were the most antisocial guys in school. They knew how to ollie the courtyard bench, but they did not know how to talk to girls—or to anyone, really.

"I actually think they'd be a good couple," Irene said. "She can yammer and he can sit there and listen—that is, unless you turn Devon down. Then *he'll* have to listen to Darcy yammering."

"So will you, if you hang with Devon at the prom," Haley said.

"Ugh, you're right. So, Haley, the fate of many

people rests in your hands. Not just Devon's prom night but mine and Shaun's too. Please say yes to Devon."

"I'll think about it," Haley said.

Irene fell to her knees and clasped her hands together in prayer. "Look at me, Haley, I'm begging you. Go to Holy Roller Records tomorrow. Three o'clock sharp. If I have to spend prom night listening to that airhead Darcy blather on about how she matched her nail polish to her tattoos, I'll end up hurting someone. That someone is likely to be Shaun. So, for Shaun's sake, if you care about his welfare at all, please go to the prom with Devon."

● ● ●

Irene has put her finger on the key: Haley's decision about the prom will affect more people than she realizes. Irene's proposition is interesting. Now Haley has to make up her mind: will Devon be her prom date?

There's something kind of romantic about setting up a signal, a rendezvous at a record store where Devon will pop the question. But some girls might be annoyed by the situation, because it gives Devon all the power. He risks nothing; Haley shoulders all the risk. If he wants to ask her to the prom, shouldn't he just ask her, rather than wait to make sure the answer will be yes first?

But then, Devon has always been risk-averse; that's

just Devon. If Haley really likes him, she'll want to go to the prom with him no matter how he asks her.

Devon's not the only prom option open to Haley. She could wait and see who else asks her—though that would mean blowing her Holy Roller deadline with Devon. Both Reese Highland and Alex Martin have dropped hints that they might consider asking Haley to the prom—and they're not demanding that she promise to say yes before they even ask.

If you think Haley should accept Irene's proposition and go to the prom with Devon, send her to HOLY ROLLER RECORDS on page 191. If you think Alex Martin would make a better prom date for Haley, go to page 194, THE TRADITIONALIST. If you think Reese Highland has had "prom date" written all over him since the day he and Haley met, go to PORCH-SWING PROPOSAL on page 189. Finally, if you think Haley would like to try her luck with the cool crowd on prom night, go to page 178, SINGING TELEGRAM.

One person's porn is another person's avant-garde dreck.

"Here we go." Annie Armstrong brought a tray of snacks into the basement, where Haley and Dave were sitting with RoBro! listening to music. "We've got dairy-free cheese spread on wheat-free crackers, carrot sticks and hummus with no garlic. Plus a glass of triple-filtered spring water for each of us. Dig in!"

Haley reached for her water glass while Dave munched a wheat-free cracker. He was allergic to practically everything and Annie had adapted to his special needs admirably. Dave was staying at the Armstrongs' house while his mother and Mr. Von were away on their honeymoon.

"So how long will your parents be in Hawaii?" Haley asked.

"They're not my parents," Dave said morosely. "At least, *he's* not. And I'm beginning to wonder about her."

Annie glanced at Haley and shook her head. Apparently Dave was still not adapting well to the recent changes in his life.

Dave acted as if nothing were wrong, bopping his head to the electronic music on the stereo. "RoBro! loves techno, of course," he said. "His favorite band is Kraftwerk."

"Never heard of them," Haley said, listening to the mechanical beeps and thumps.

"They were a German band in the seventies," Dave said. "I never heard of them either until Mr. Von turned me on to them."

"He said you can call him Rick now, remember?" Annie said.

"I remember," Dave said. "I choose to ignore that."

"It's interesting that RoBro!'s favorite band would be a Mr. Von pick," Haley said. "Does that mean you're warming up to him?"

"No," Dave said firmly. "Don't you read the Internet? Mr. Von is a pervert."

"I don't believe those rumors, do you, Annie?" Haley said.

"No," Annie said. "Mr. Von is kind of eccentric, but I've never seen him do anything perverted. But the PTA and the school board are freaking. I heard he's this close to being fired."

"Who do you think is behind those rumors?" Haley asked.

Annie shrugged. "Probably some kid who's failing art. But who fails art? Isn't it impossible to fail art?"

"Nothing is impossible," Dave said. "Including Mr. Von being a pervert."

"But why do you say that?" Haley asked Dave. She was getting a funny feeling about this. Dave was the first person she'd talked to who actually took the "Mr. Von, porn star" gossip seriously. Why would that be?

"Because it's true," Dave said. "I have proof."

Haley gasped. "It's you! You started the rumors!"

"I told you, they're not rumors," Dave said. "This is cold, hard fact. I'll show you."

He disappeared upstairs. "He must have gone to his room to get something," Annie said. "Mom's letting him sleep in the guest room. I sneak in at night for a few kisses, but he won't let things go farther than that. He doesn't want to upset my parents after they've been so nice to him."

A few minutes later Dave returned with a computer

disk in his hand. "The original was on Super-8 film, but I transferred it to DVD. Check this out—and set your phasers to stunned."

He slipped the DVD into the computer and a black-and-white image appeared on the screen. A very young Mr. Von—he looked about college-aged, with long hair and a mustache—sat in a hot tub with two young women. Superimposed credits appeared over the image:

THREESOME
An Ontological Exploration
Written and Directed by Richard Von

"Is he—naked?" Annie asked, peering at the screen.

"Totally. Naked," Dave said.

"But he's in a hot tub," Haley pointed out. "I mean, doesn't everybody bathe naked?"

The women were topless, but the water pretty much covered everything interesting. In fact, Mr. Von could have had a bathing suit on—there was no way of knowing.

"Donna, you are perfection," Mr. Von said to one of the girls in a stiff voice.

"Kathy, you are perfection," Donna said to the other girl.

"Rick, you are perfection," Kathy said to Mr. Von.

"We are all perfection," Mr. Von said.

"If this is porn it must be the most boring porn on earth," Annie said. "Not that I'd know."

"Wait," Dave said. "Watch this part."

"We are perfect, therefore God exists," Mr. Von declared. "Our perfection is proof. Let us stand up and show the world the proof of God's existence." All three of them stood up in the hot tub and shouted, "We are proof that God exists!"

"Well, they're definitely naked," Haley said.

"Definitely," Annie said.

"I told you," Dave said.

The film flashed to a new scene. Mr. Von wore some kind of pink feathered costume. Kathy was wearing a black leotard and tickling him with a feather.

"Is that a pink chicken suit?" Haley asked.

"Rooster," Dave said. "See the red comb on top of his head?"

Haley sat through a few more minutes of the movie, which was clearly Mr. Von's youthful attempt at making an experimental art film. "Dave, this isn't porn. It's just a bad art-school movie."

"What are you talking about?" Dave protested. "Didn't you see how naked they were? My stepfather naked with two girls! This is the filthiest movie I've ever seen!"

"It may be the filthiest movie *you've* ever seen, Dave," Annie said. "But it's not porn."

"You've got to come clean and take back all the

terrible things you said about Mr. Von on the Internet," Haley said. "Or his career will be ruined! Think about your mother—would that make her happy?"

Dave crossed his arms over his chest and pouted. "It's mystifying to me what makes her happy. I never would have thought marrying *him* would make her happy, yet here we are, waiting out their honeymoon at the Armstrongs' house like abandoned puppies."

"Speak for yourself," Annie said. "*My* parents would never leave me alone to go on a cushy sex trip."

"Annie!" Haley nudged Annie with her foot. "You're not helping." There was still some tension between Annie and Dave, she could see.

"I'm just trying to be open and honest," Annie said. "That's what Dave needs most of all—to open up."

"Maybe you're right," Haley said. She tapped RoBro!, who clanged slightly. "Dave, let's talk about the real issue here. The twenty-pound robot in the room. Let's talk about RoBro!"

Dave's lips trembled and beads of sweat broke out on his pimply forehead. "RoBro!? What about him?"

"You know he's not your real brother, don't you?" Annie asked.

Dave stared down at his hands. "Of course I know that. I'm not an imbecile."

"Then why are you so attached to him?" Haley asked.

"Duh, it's obvious," Annie said. "Any therapist with the least bit of training in Freudian theory could tell you that he's projecting his need for a father on RoBro! because his real father rejected him."

"Annie," Haley said, kicking her again. "Any therapist with the least bit of training in anything would also tell you to let the patient answer the question. And Dave is the patient, not you."

"That's okay, Annie," Dave said. "It helped me to hear you say it out loud. I went looking for my real father, and when I found him, he didn't want me. Then my mother told me she was marrying Mr. Von. . . . A stepfather would have been bad enough, but the fact that he's a teacher at my school made everything a hundred times worse, and I felt like she didn't care about my feelings. No one did. Except Annie, but she can be a little brusque."

"What!" Annie looked offended.

"I'm sorry, Annie, but you can be. I'm crazy about you, pumpkin cake, you know that. But you said to be open, so I'm being open."

"Annie, you know he's right," Haley said. "Let it go."

Annie rolled her eyes. "I'm just honest. I say what I think. If the truth is too harsh for you . . ."

Haley gave Annie another kick, less gently this time.

"So I thought I'd make my own family," Dave

finished. "A brother, since I never had one. I could make him exactly the way I wanted him. He'd look up to me and never abandon me like my parents. . . ."

He didn't cry, but he did get sweatier, almost as if the tears came out of his forehead instead of his eyes.

"I know it looks ridiculous, talking to RoBro! as if he's really alive, taking him everywhere," Dave said. "But it made me feel better. It helped me get through the wedding and everything else."

Haley patted Dave's arm. "It's okay, Dave. We all have our own ways of coping." She suppressed a wave of nausea at the realization that she sounded exactly like her mother. But she felt sorry for Dave. He'd just been through some major family transitions and it had clearly taken a toll on him.

"I have an idea," Annie said. "Let's change the subject."

"But maybe Dave isn't finished talking," Haley protested.

"No, I'm finished," Dave said.

"Let's talk about something fun," Annie said. "Let's talk about the prom."

"What about the prom?" Haley asked warily, suspecting Annie might have matchmaking on her mind.

"Well, obviously Dave and I are going together," Annie began. "Though Dave refuses to wear the tux I picked out for him."

"I don't see why I can't wear a Storm Trooper uniform," Dave said. "In intergalactic etiquette it's considered formal wear."

"Our prom is taking place on planet Earth, not the Death Star," Annie said. "What about you, Haley? Do you have a date yet?"

"Not yet," Haley said. "If you're hoping to stick me with that kid in your math class whose glasses are taped together, you are sorely mistaken."

"What? No." Annie laughed lightly. "I know you better than that. I was just wondering what you would say if Alex asked you to go with him."

"Alex?" Haley echoed. That was another story. "Does he want to ask me?"

"It's a possibility," Annie said. "A strong possibility. Say yes, Haley! Then you can hang with us at the prom."

Haley glanced at RoBro! "Him too?"

"Yes," Dave said.

"No," Annie said. "Sorry, Dave, but RoBro! stays home. Nobody takes their little brother to the prom. You know that."

● ● ●

It's time for Haley to make up her mind. What kind of prom does she want to have? It's not just a matter of who will be her date; the boy she goes with affects which social clique she spends the evening with. So who will it be?

If you think Haley would love to be asked to the prom by Alex Martin, go to page 194, THE TRADITION-ALIST. If you think Haley would rather spend the big night with the most popular kids in school, no matter who her date is, go to page 178, SINGING TELEGRAM. If you think Haley wants to go with Reese Highland more than anyone else—and wants it so badly she's willing to ask him herself—go to page 186, ASK REESE.

SINGING TELEGRAM

Some surprises are romantic, but others are just scary.

"**A**hem. Excuse me, everyone. Sorry to interrupt your free period but this is important."

Haley looked up as Johnny Lane's voice blared out of the school loudspeakers. It was a warm late-spring afternoon, and Haley was enjoying the sun with Coco, Cecily, Whitney and Sasha.

"What's he doing?" Sasha grinned, surprised to hear her boyfriend over the PA system.

"This is Sasha Lewis radio," Johnny said. "All Sasha, all the time." He cleared his throat and strummed a few chords on his guitar. "Sasha, this is for you."

Sasha blushed as all eyes in the courtyard turned to her. "I swear I had no idea he was going to do this."

Johnny began to sing.

> "Sasha, you're my world
> You're more than just a girl to me
> I want to take you dancing every day.
> Sasha baby, won't you go with me
> Sasha baby, go to the prom with me
> Say yes, Sasha baby, say yes, say yes
> I want to spin you around in your fancy dress
> Say yes, Sasha baby, say yes."

The courtyard burst into applause as Johnny said, "Sasha, that's my way of asking, will you go to the prom with me? Please say yes. I'll see you soon. This is Johnny Lane, signing off."

"Wow," Haley said. "That's got to be the best way any girl has ever been asked to the prom in the history of high school."

"It was pretty amazing," Sasha said, beaming.

"What are you going to say?" Whitney asked.

"Duh," Coco said. "How can she turn him down now?"

"Here he comes," Cecily said.

All eyes were on Johnny as he walked across the

courtyard and made straight for Sasha. He wore his usual tight black jeans and untucked T-shirt under a leather jacket, sunglasses on, his guitar strapped over his back.

"He's so cool," Whitney muttered.

He reached down and took Sasha's hand. "What do you say?"

Sasha threw her arms around him. "Yes! Yes, of course!"

Everyone clapped and cheered again as they kissed. It was so romantic, Haley thought. The rest of the boys in school would be hard-pressed to top that.

But that didn't stop them from trying. A few hours later, the girls gathered at the track field for Cecily's big meet against Ridgewood. After she ran— and won—her biggest race of the day, the electronic scoreboard flashed her name and time, and the standings. Then it suddenly went blank, and in huge red letters flashed: CECILY, YOU MAKE MY HEART RACE. WILL YOU GO TO THE PROM WITH ME? DREW.

Cecily was still catching her breath as she stared in amazement at the message on the board. The crowd started chanting, "Say yes! Say yes! Yes! Yes! Yes!" Drew made his way down the bleachers with a big bouquet of flowers in his arms. He presented them to Cecily, who was panting and beaming in her running shorts.

"Yes!" she shouted, and the crowd went wild.

The scoreboard graphics flashed hearts and fireworks as Cecily and Drew kissed.

"That was the most amazing prom proposal I've ever seen," Whitney gushed. "I wish something like that would happen to me."

"Me too," Haley said. The only problem was, she didn't know which boy she wished would ask her. But a romantic gesture like that from almost any boy would be wonderful, she thought.

"Anything's possible," Coco said mysteriously. "Wait and see."

Little did Coco know that she was next.

The next afternoon, after the last bell rang, Haley and Coco were leaving Spanish class and heading out to the parking lot to go home for the day. But Spencer Eton had other plans.

"Do you hear music?" Coco asked as they pushed through the front door of the school building.

"Oh my God," Haley said. The music blasted them now, classic funky dance tunes played by a DJ in the parking lot. There were streamers and balloons tied to the cars and five spaces cleared for a makeshift dance floor. A banner draped over the lot said, in bright metallic blue letters, COCO DE CLERQ, THIS PARTY'S FOR YOU.

"What the—?" Coco stared at the sign, stunned. Haley had never seen her so flustered. "What's going on?"

The school building emptied as everyone

gathered in the parking lot to dance and talk. Then the DJ segued into "You're the First, the Last, My Everything" as Spencer rode into the scene in a white stretch limo, his head poking out of the sunroof. He wore a sleek black tuxedo and carried an armful of red roses. He jumped onto the roof of the car, took the microphone from the DJ and said, "Coco De Clerq, you are my first, my last, my everything. When I look in your eyes, I think I'm in love."

A big "awww" went up from the crowd.

"There's a big dance coming up," Spencer said. "I think they call it the prom. Dances aren't usually my thing, but Coco, if you'll go with me"—he dropped to one knee and held out the roses to her—"I promise to make it the greatest night of your life."

Coco's cheeks flamed with excitement and pleasure. She took the roses from Spencer, crowned him with them like a queen knighting a courtier and kissed him. "Yes," she said. "I wouldn't go with anyone else."

The DJ turned up the music and everybody spent two hours after school partying in the parking lot.

"This just keeps getting better and better," Whitney said. "What's next, skywriting?"

A clown carrying a huge bunch of multicolored balloons threaded his way through the crowd. "Whitney Klein!" he shouted. "I'm looking for Whitney Klein!"

"Ooh! That's me!" Whitney jumped up and

waved to the clown, who handed her the gigantic bunch of balloons.

"These are for you," he said.

"Who are they from?" Whitney asked.

"You gotta pop them to find out," the clown said. "Here, use this." He gave her a big straight pin with a heart on one end. "Have fun."

Whitney popped the balloons one by one. "There must be a hundred of them," she said. Students began to gather around to watch. Finally Whitney popped the one red balloon and a note fluttered to the ground. She reached down to pick it up. Her name was written on the outside of an envelope.

"Open it!" someone said.

She opened the envelope, read the note and squealed with delight. She tossed the note to Haley, then started jumping up and down and hugging her.

Haley read the note. *Dear Whitney, I would be honored if you went to the prom with me. Will you say yes? Reese.*

Haley smiled on the outside but inside her heart sank. Reese was really asking Whitney to the prom. Haley realized that deep down, she'd been hoping Reese would refuse to go along with Coco's plan. But everything was falling into place, just as Coco wanted it.

"That's great, Whit," Haley said.

"Where is he? Reese, where are you?" Whitney jumped up onto the bumper of a car, scanning the crowd for Reese. When she spotted him she yelled, "Reese! Reese! Over here!"

Reese jogged over. Whitney leaped into his arms, nearly knocking him on his butt. "Yes!" she cried. "Yes, I'll totally be your prom date!"

"Awesome," Reese said. "Did you like the balloons?"

"I loved them!"

Haley hung out at the party a little longer, hoping someone would make a dramatic prom proposal to her, but nothing else happened that afternoon. She went home feeling dejected. All her friends had been asked to the prom in the most romantic ways possible, and she was still left without a date. The prom was fast approaching. *Maybe I won't go,* she thought as she fell asleep that night. *I don't want to be the only dateless wonder there.*

The next day, Coco sat next to Haley in Spanish class. "Wasn't that party yesterday incredible?" Coco said. "It's the sweetest thing Spencer has ever done for me. I think I've finally tamed him."

"It was amazing, all right," Haley said.

Just then the classroom door burst open and a six-foot-tall gorilla—or rather, a man in a gorilla costume—stepped in.

"My name is Matthew Graham," the gorilla sang. "Some people say I'm a ham. I don't even go to your school, but there's a Hillsdale girl I think is cool, and

I want to take her to your prom. Oh Haley, Haley Miller, won't you go to the prom with me?"

Ms. Frick's Spanish class applauded the gorilla, who took a bow. Then all eyes turned to Haley. "Well?" the gorilla said. "What answer should I deliver to Matt?"

● ● ●

The bad boys of Hillsdale have certainly stepped it up a notch for prom night—maybe they're still trying to make up for their misbehavior during winter break. That's a distant memory now for most of the Coco clique. Coco, Cecily, Sasha and even Whitney are seeing their fondest prom dreams come true, with the boys they like best courting them in style. Haley's the only one with reason to hesitate. She's not sure whether Matt is asking her because he really likes her or because Coco and Spencer fixed it up. And even if Matt's crazy for Haley, how does she feel about him? On the other hand, what other choice does she have?

If you think Haley should accept her fate and go to the prom with Matt, go to page 201, FINAL FITTING. If you think Haley should fight the power and find a way to go to the prom with Reese, no matter what she has to do or whose feelings she has to hurt, go to page 186, ASK REESE.

Even good intentions can sometimes backfire.

It's just wrong, Haley said to herself over and over in her room. She was so obsessed with the idea of Reese going to the prom with Whitney that she couldn't think about anything else. She barely ate dinner, couldn't concentrate on her homework, couldn't think about anything else but the prom. The idea of going with Matt didn't bother her as much as the utter wrongness of Whitney and Reese. Who did Coco think she was? How could she play God with

people's lives like this? Reese had never been interested in Whitney, Haley felt sure of it.

Haley's pulse raced. She was starting to panic.
This is my prom we're talking about, she thought. *It's
a big deal. I can't just accept what fate—or Coco—
hands me. I've got to take matters into my own hands
or I'll be miserable. Maybe I'll even regret it for the rest
of my life.*

Maybe I should talk to him, she thought. *He can't
be serious about taking Whitney to the prom.* Maybe
he wanted to get out of it as much as Haley did—he
was just looking for an excuse.

If that's the case, I'll give him one, Haley decided.

She reached for her cell before she could change
her mind, and punched in Reese's number. "Reese?"
she said when he answered. "Hey, it's Haley."

"Hi, Haley." Was that a hint of wariness in his
voice? She ignored it and plowed ahead.

"Listen, I was thinking about the prom," she
said. "And, I mean, we can't let Coco push us around
like this. I know you don't really want to take
Whitney—"

"How do you know that?" Reese asked. "Can you
read my mind?"

"Well, no," Haley said. "I just figured that, given
the choice, you'd rather go with me. I mean, we're a
much more logical couple than you and Whitney."

"I don't know." Haley suddenly detected a

coldness in his voice that gave her chills. "Maybe I don't believe in logic when it comes to couples."

Desperate, she took one last plunge. "Reese, I called to ask you to go to the prom with me. We could have a lot of fun together. What do you say?"

"You know what, Haley? I say no. I asked Whitney and I'm going to the prom with Whitney. I don't go back on my word, and I don't enjoy hurting people's feelings for my own selfish reasons. Thanks anyway."

He hung up, leaving Haley in shock. When the shock wore off, she felt like banging her head against the wall. She was ruined. Once Matt heard about this, he'd retract his offer to take her to the prom, and she'd have no date. *I might as well stay home in bed that night,* she thought. *I might as well stay in bed for the rest of my life.*

● ● ●

Big mistake. Haley should have known that Reese is too honorable to ditch Whitney for her, whether he likes her better or not. But now he doesn't like Haley at all. She came off too pushy and pushed Reese—and her whole prom night—right out the door.

That's what you get when you play around at the top of the social heap. She should have just accepted her fate and gone with Matt. She might have had a good time. Maybe next time she'll know better.

Hang your head and go back to page 1.

PORCH-SWING PROPOSAL

Sometimes the best plan of action is no action at all.

Reese knocked on the Millers' door on Sunday afternoon, just as he'd promised. Haley'd been wondering since breakfast what he wanted to talk to her about, though she had an idea.

He smiled awkwardly when she answered the door. "Hey," he said. "Got a minute?"

"Sure," she said. "Want to sit on the porch swing?"

"Great."

It was a beautiful, warm late-spring afternoon.

Haley sat beside Reese on the porch swing and rocked it gently. "What's up?"

She turned and looked at him head-on. He swallowed nervously. "I had a whole speech planned, but instead I think I'll just go for it," he said. "Haley Miller, would you like to go to the prom with me?"

Just as she'd suspected. And she had her answer ready.

● ● ●

Reese has finally taken the plunge and asked Haley to the prom. Now she has to decide once and for all if he's the one for her.

Coco has made it clear that she wants Reese to go with Whitney, and Haley with Matt Graham. If Haley says yes to Reese, Coco is bound to be displeased. Displeasing Coco takes courage and rarely comes without consequences.

If you think Haley should throw caution to the wind, screw Coco and say yes to Reese, go to page 198, MOMENT WITH MOM. If you think Haley shouldn't risk Coco's wrath, have her go along with Coco's original plan and go to the prom with Matt Graham on page 201, FINAL FITTING. If you think Haley would rather stay away from this sticky situation altogether and go with Alex Martin instead, go to page 209, BOUTIQUE BAROQUE.

HOLY ROLLER RECORDS

It takes a special girl to
be charmed by eighties
hair metal.

At 2:45 Haley hopped into her car—an embarrassing yellow heap that had once belonged to her grandmother and looked it—and drove across town to Holy Roller Records. It was a ten-minute drive, which still left her five minutes' cushion to make sure she was there by three o'clock, Devon's witching hour. Irene had told her that if she didn't show up by three, Devon would think she didn't like him and ask Darcy Podowski to the prom instead.

Haley still wasn't sure who she wanted to go to

the prom with, but she wanted to give Devon the chance to ask her. She figured she'd see how she felt when she heard the words come out of his mouth. She didn't quite believe he really planned on asking her—he was usually too passive and wishy-washy to do something so definite.

She parked in front of the shop and looked for Devon through the plate glass window. There he was, flipping through a stack of vintage LPs. He looked up when she walked in.

"Hey," he said, as if he'd been expecting her. "I picked out something for you." He pulled a record from the stack. The cover showed a garish eighties hair band posing pretentiously in spandex outfits.

"Whitesnake?" Haley said. "You picked out a Whitesnake record for me?"

"This is a special Whitesnake record," Devon said.

Haley took the album and turned it over. On the back, the lead singer had a speech bubble drawn with black marker coming out of his mouth. It said, *Want to hit up the prom, baby?*

Haley burst out laughing. Devon laughed too. "This has to be the funniest prom offer ever," Haley said. "The question is, do I get to go with you, or do I have to go with the lead singer of Whitesnake?"

● ● ●

Well, he did it—Devon finally asked Haley to the prom. Of course, she never did get to hear the words come out

of his mouth, since, typical Devon, he made them come out of Whitesnake's mouth instead. Still, it is pretty funny, and very Devon.

Now Haley has a choice: she can say yes to Devon and Whitesnake, or she can go with someone else. She may get an offer from Alex Martin, who may not be as funny as Devon. But then, is funny what she wants in a prom date? It's up to you to decide.

If you think Haley's charmed by Devon's proposal, have her say yes and go to page 205, JACK'S JACKPOT, to pick out a dress. If you think Haley would rather have a more traditional prom date, send her shopping for something elegant to wear on page 209, BOUTIQUE BAROQUE.

THE TRADITIONALIST

Even smart boys need a cheat sheet once in a while.

"Haley, someone's here to see you." Joan Miller knocked on Haley's bedroom door, then opened it before Haley had a chance to say "Come in." An annoying habit of her mother's.

"Come in," Haley said when her mother was already in, just to make a point. "Who is it?"

"Go downstairs and see." Joan had a cryptic smile on her face. Haley wondered what was up. She'd heard the doorbell ring, but that was fifteen minutes ago. What was this visitor doing with her parents all that time if he—or she—was here to see *her*?

Haley went downstairs and found Alex waiting in the front hall, a dozen long-stemmed red roses in his arms. He looked even more adorable than usual dressed in a sports jacket over a button-down shirt, his brown hair boyishly parted on the side and combed into place.

"Alex, hey, what's—"

Before she could finish her question, Alex got down on one knee and pulled a piece of lined yellow legal paper from his jacket pocket.

"Haley," he said, reading from the paper, "you and I have known each other for almost a year now. When we first met, I took one look at you and thought you were beautiful. I still think you're the most beautiful girl in school. But the more I get to know you, the more I admire your intelligence, integrity and character. You have elegance and style. I'm sure you have been bombarded with boys asking you to the prom, and I can only hope this humble attempt does not come too late. And so I officially ask: Haley, would you do me the honor of accompanying me to the Hillsdale High School prom this year?"

Haley was touched. He had gone to all that trouble to write out his proposal, and to bring it with him to read to make sure he got it right, down to each word. That was so Alex.

"If you're hesitating because you're wondering if

it's okay with your parents, don't worry, I already asked their permission to escort you, and they said it was all right with them," Alex informed her.

"It's true, he did," Joan said. She was standing on the stairs watching the whole thing. "He even offered to let us interview him to make sure he was a suitable prom date for you, but we told him we felt the decision was really up to you, not us."

"Wow, thanks for giving me permission to choose my own prom date." Haley couldn't hide the hint of sarcasm in her voice.

Alex was still on one knee and starting to wobble. "Please stand up," Haley said. "That looks very uncomfortable."

"Thank you." Alex rose to his feet, offering her the flowers. She took them and sniffed them. They smelled fresh and wonderful.

"I await your response," Alex said.

● ● ●

It's do-or-die time for Haley now. No more hemming and hawing. After Alex's elaborate, traditional proposal, he deserves a definite yes-or-no answer.

And there is something wonderful about the old-fashioned way he does things. It's clear that he not only likes Haley a lot but respects her, too. And he knows how to make a mother happy. But does he take the traditionalist thing too far? Some girls might not like a boy who involves her parents in her dating decisions. In fact, most girls would rather leave their parents' opinions out of it.

As Alex pointed out, Haley has other options. She could go to the prom with hottie Reese Highland, or with intense, arty Devon McKnight. Each boy promises to give her a unique prom experience. All Haley has to do is choose.

If you think Haley would like to go to the prom the old-fashioned way, with Alex, go to page 209, BOUTIQUE BAROQUE. If you think It Boy Reese is the one and only date for her, go to page 198, MOMENT WITH MOM. If you think Haley wants to bust out of the norm and have an unconventional prom night with the unconventional Devon, go to page 205, JACK'S JACKPOT.

It's one of the biggest nights of a girl's life. Don't screw it up.

MOMENT WITH MOM

Like mother, like daughter—
to a point.

"You're going to have a wonderful time tonight," Joan Miller said through the bathroom door. Haley was in her mother's room getting ready for her big prom night. "I always thought Reese was the perfect boy for you. He's got a good head on his shoulders, and he obviously cares about you a lot. We're lucky that he happens to live right next door."

Haley didn't answer—she was too busy staring at her reflection in the bathroom mirror. She'd decided to wear the very dress Joan had worn to her own prom, a simple cotton eyelet dress with smocked bodice and an off-the-shoulder ruffle. It fit her so perfectly it was almost spooky. She tried to imagine her mother at seventeen in this same dress.

"Everything okay in there?" Joan asked. "How does it fit?"

Haley opened the door and stepped into the bedroom. "Ta-da." She spun around so that her mother could see.

Joan gasped. "It's incredible. So perfect on you. I thought we might have to let out the hem a bit, but no. . . ." Joan's eyes were wet. "It's almost like seeing a ghost of myself. Except you're prettier than I ever was, honey."

"That's not true," Haley said. "I've seen the pictures."

Joan hugged Haley tight. "I can't believe my little girl is going to the prom. How did you grow up so fast?"

"It didn't feel that fast to me," Haley said, and they both laughed, wiping tears from their eyes.

"Wait—I got you something." Joan opened the top drawer of her dresser. "The gown is a little plain, so I thought you might want to dress it up with this." She gave Haley a long velvet box, and Haley opened it. Inside was a string of pearls.

"My parents gave them to me when I graduated from high school," Joan said. "I want you to have them now."

"Mom . . . they're beautiful!" Haley felt so choked with emotion she could hardly speak. "Thank you."

Her mother fastened the pearls around Haley's neck. "There. They look gorgeous on you. And I'm sure Reese will give you a corsage, so that will add a splash of color to the dress. You'll be the belle of the prom. Do they do that whole Prom Queen and King thing here?"

"I don't think so," Haley said. "Thank goodness."

"Yes, it is a little hokey." The doorbell rang. "Is that Reese already?"

"I'd better put on a little makeup," Haley said. She'd decided to wear her hair simple, straight and down, so all that took was a quick swipe with the brush. "Tell him I'll be down in ten minutes."

"Don't worry, I'll keep him busy," Joan said. She gave Haley one last hug. "Have a great time tonight, honey. I'll see you downstairs."

Haley went to her room to do her makeup—not too much, since she was going for a natural look. When she was finished, she slipped on her new white sandals, took one final mirror-check and went downstairs to meet Reese.

●　●　●

Haley's prom is off to a good start with a warm and fuzzy moment with Mom. Now the real fun begins. Turn to page 213 to see Haley off to the PROM WITH REESE.

FINAL FITTING

Girl bonding only works if everyone participates.

"Sasha, hold still," Whitney snapped as she zipped her stepsister into the electric blue prom dress she'd made for her. "Haley, how does yours fit?"

Haley stepped out of the dressing room in her silver-gray silk WK original. "Perfect!" Whitney said. "I just need to tighten the straps a little and it will be good to go." Whitney had practically sewn it to her body, so it ought to fit well. Haley hoped her prom date, Matt Graham, would like it. She didn't see any reason why he wouldn't. It was a long sleeveless gown with a deep V, a slightly flaring skirt and a wide sash around the waist. Haley's skin and hair gleamed against the metallic fabric.

"Are you kidding?" Coco strutted around Whitney's design studio in her custom-made fuchsia dress, nitpicking about the little ways it wasn't working for her. Now she turned her lasers on Haley. "Do you really want to go to the prom looking like that? That dress adds ten pounds to your figure."

"What? What are you talking about?" Haley checked herself in the mirror, but to her eye the dress looked fine on her.

"Look how it puckers here." Coco tugged at the fabric at Haley's hip. "And the way it bunches at the belly. Every snag in the fabric adds inches to your silhouette. Of course, if you want to look like Rosie O'Donnell, that's your business."

"Haley, don't listen to her." Cecily was relaxing on the couch in her own WK creation, a stunning gold halter gown. "You look gorgeous and not the least bit heavy."

Whitney studied the dress with a critical eye. "What are you talking about, Coco? Haley's dress fits perfectly. You can't avoid a little pucker here and there, but the eye adjusts for it. You don't want to wear a skintight dress to the prom—that's totally tacky."

"I just thought Haley should know the truth

while she's still here and there's a chance you could fix the problems," Coco said.

"Are you crazy?" Whitney said. "There's no time to fix anything. The prom is in two hours."

"There are no problems as far as I'm concerned," Haley assured Whitney. And it was true, the dress looked fine to her—at least it had until Coco started criticizing it. Now Haley felt less than sure about it. Maybe she really did look fat. Was it too late to change? Stupid Coco. By now Haley knew it was just her way of undermining Haley's confidence, probably because Coco herself was feeling nervous. Coco couldn't help it—it was just her personality. So why did Haley still let it get to her?

"Haley, Matt's jaw is going to drop when he sees you," Sasha said, turning in front of the mirror.

"Yeah, he'll be stunned at how chunky his date looks," Coco said.

"That's not what I meant at all," Sasha said. "He'll be stunned at how lovely she is! Coco, we're trying to have a girl bonding moment here and you're ruining it."

Whitney surveyed her friends in the dresses she had designed and made herself. Her own dress, a pink satin number, hung from a fitting mannequin nearby. She looked satisfied. "You all look amazing, and nothing Coco says can change my mind," she pronounced with uncharacteristic firmness.

"Thank you for making these dresses for us, Whit," Cecily said. "They really are incredibly chic."

"If you could just shorten my hem another quarter inch, Whit," Coco said. "I promise after that I'll stop nitpicking."

● ● ●

Coco's nerves are getting to her, and as usual she's taking it out on those around her. Haley has nothing to worry about, dress-wise. She looks fabulous. She's understandably nervous, though, since her prom date, Matt Graham, is something of an unknown quantity. You never know with Matt; he could be charming or he could be a jerk. To see what happens at the PROM WITH MATT, go to page 220.

JACK'S JACKPOT

Vintage shopping requires
a keen eye.

"Is he in there?" Haley waited on the sidewalk out-side Jack's Vintage Clothing while Irene scouted the store for signs of Devon.

"No," Irene said. "That girl's working. The one with the nose ring. I told you he was off today."

The coast clear, Haley went inside with Irene. She was shopping for a prom dress, and she didn't want Devon, her date, to see what she picked out be-fore the big night. But since Devon worked at Jack's and Jack's was where Haley hoped to find her dream dress, things got tricky.

The nose-ring girl looked up when they walked in. "Hi. Let me know if you need any help."

"We're looking for prom dresses," Irene said.

"We just got a big shipment in yesterday." The girl pointed to a rack near the dressing room. "Lots of cute stuff."

"Thanks." Haley made a beeline for the rack. Before she even got there Irene zipped past her and pounced on a violet dress with a tulle skirt.

"Look at this!" Irene held the gown up against her body. "Fantabulous! Please be a small, please be a small. . . ." She checked the label. "A small!"

"Try it on, spaz." Haley flipped through the rack while Irene went into the changing room. She pawed through a lot of yawn-inducing poufy dresses from the eighties in Day-Glo colors before she got to a small cache of good stuff: sleek, high-fashion designer gowns from the sixties through the nineties at rock-bottom prices. She pulled out three dresses to try on. Irene popped out of the changing room in the violet tulle.

"What do you think?" Irene asked.

"It completes you," Haley said. "Do you like it?"

"I love it!" Irene cried. "I can't believe it was that easy to find a prom dress. What have you got there?"

Haley showed her the three dresses she'd picked out: a long, straight midnight blue column with a rhinestone neckline; a sexy, stretchy black dress that appeared to be made out of sewn-together elastic bandages; and a silk psychedelic-print mini with bell sleeves.

"Ooh, tough call," Irene said. "You've got Princess Grace, Cindy Crawford circa 1990 or swinging Goldie Hawn in her peak free-spirit years. Let's see how they look on you."

Haley tried on the bandage dress first. It was figure-hugging, like a long girdle, slit up the back, and showed off every curve.

"Yowza!" Irene said when Haley stepped out of the dressing room. "The boys' eyes will pop out of their heads when they see this one."

"I think it's a little too too," Haley said.

"I agree," Irene said. "It looks amazing, but it's not you. Besides, you don't want people drooling on you all night."

Haley changed into the psychedelic mini and modeled it for Irene.

"Adorable," Irene said. "I think you should get it. But it's not fancy enough for the prom."

"Agreed," Haley said. She changed into the midnight blue column, which she'd had a gut feeling would turn out to be her favorite all along. It fit perfectly, skimming along her body without clinging or revealing too much. It was simple, but the rhinestone neckline added glamour.

"You saved the best for last," Irene said. "That's the one."

"I really love it," Haley said. "And it's comfortable, too. Do you think Devon will like it?"

"I think he'd love you in a plastic garbage bag," Irene said. "But the artist in him will approve of this dress for sure. It's elegant, yet fun."

"Perfect." The girls paid for their dresses and went out for cappuccinos to celebrate.

● ● ●

Haley's found the perfect prom dress. Now the question is: will she have the perfect prom night? To find out how things go, check out PROM WITH DEVON on page 227.

BOUTIQUE BAROQUE

When it comes to big events, the dress makes the girl.

"Look at this one." Haley held out a stunning red satin gown for her mother to see. "And this one." An ethereal pale blue chiffon. "Oh my God, look at this one!" A full-skirted ball gown with a subtle floral pattern. "They're all so beautiful!"

"They certainly are," Joan said, frowning at the price tags.

Joan had brought Haley to Mimi's Boutique to buy a designer prom dress, her treat. Mimi's was the most elegant shop in town and carried all the most sophisticated clothes, with price tags to match. Haley was overwhelmed; each dress was more gorgeous than the last. How would she ever pick just one?

"Mom," she said. "I just want to tell you how much I appreciate this—your buying a dress for me. It's really generous of you."

"I'm glad to do it, honey," Joan said. "The prom is a big moment for you. I want you to enjoy it."

Haley truly was grateful: her mother's generosity was the only way Haley would ever be able to afford a really spectacular gown. And since she was going to the prom with Alex, a mature senior, she wanted something sophisticated. Alex was going off to Georgetown in the fall, and Haley worried that he'd start to think of her as the hometown kid he left behind, rather than the smart girl-on-the-rise she wanted to be.

Mimi, the owner of the shop, appeared from the back and sized Haley up with an appraising glance. "A lovely girl. I think I have the perfect dress for you." She flipped through the rack until she came to a long, slinky evening gown, strapless, in black and white.

Haley gasped. "I love it."

"I don't know," Joan said. "It's very sophisticated for a high school prom."

"Try it on just to see how it fits," Mimi said.

Haley took it into the dressing room. The gown

slipped on like a second skin. Mimi stepped in to zip up the back. "That dress was made for you," she said.

Haley came out to model for her mother. "Oh, Haley," Joan said. Tears welled up in her eyes. "I can't get over how grown up you look. . . ."

"And with her hair up . . ." Mimi twisted Haley's auburn hair and loosely pinned it up. "Just think."

Haley turned in front of the three-way mirror, admiring the fit of the dress. It transformed her from a New Jersey teenager into a young woman of the world. It was as if she looked into the mirror and saw her own future self.

"How much is it?" Joan asked.

Haley reached for the price tag, then blanched. "Wow. It's too much, Mom."

"Let me see." Joan glanced at the price and let out a little laugh. "That *is* a lot." She stepped back to take in her daughter again. "But you look so amazing in it. Do you really like it?"

"I'm crazy about it," Haley said. "But I can't ask you to spend that much on me—"

"Hush," Joan said. "Never mind. You know what? I want to buy that dress for you. It's worth a splurge."

"Oh, Mom—really?"

Joan nodded, and Haley threw her arms around her mother's neck in a big, happy hug. "You're the best!"

"I'm glad to do it, sweetheart. You're growing up so fast. . . ." She wiped away a tear.

"Mom, don't start crying now. I haven't even applied to colleges yet."

"I know, I can't help it. . . ."

● ● ●

Haley has found the perfect dress for an evening with Alex—something that shows off her sophisticated side. Alex isn't the only one who admires Haley's newfound maturity: her mother seems blown away by it, to the point of tears. But that's a mother for you.

Now that she has the dress, how will the rest of prom night go? To find out, turn to page 233, PROM WITH ALEX.

PROM WITH REESE

When something clicks, you know it.

"Wow," Haley gasped as she and Reese walked into the Grand Ballroom at the Hillsdale Heights Hotel. "I can't believe this is the old HHH."

"The prom committee really transformed the place," Reese agreed.

Dressed in their prom finery, Haley in her mother's classic gown and Reese in a traditional black tuxedo, they stepped from the streets of Hillsdale into a twinkling wonderland. Wisely eschewing a theme this year, with a mandate from the juniors and seniors to "just make it cool," the prom committee had simply darkened the ballroom, lit it with candles, glowing lights and warm spotlights, added some vines and flowers and replaced the ceiling with a starry sky.

"There's the Coco mafia," Reese said, pointing to a large round table in the center of the room. "Let's go check in."

They walked over to the cool table: Coco and Spencer, Drew and Cecily, Sasha and Johnny and Whitney and Matt. Each table sat eight, so there was no room left for Reese and Haley.

"Everybody's looking sharp tonight," Reese said, surveying the good-looking crowd.

"Sorry there's no room for you guys," Coco said, sounding not all that sorry.

"We can squish over," Whitney suggested.

"No, that's all right," Reese said. "I want Haley to myself tonight." He took her arm. "How about a quiet table for two in the corner?"

"Sounds great. See you guys on the dance floor!" Haley said as she and Reese walked away.

"You didn't mind not sitting with them, did you?" Reese asked.

"Not at all," Haley said. It was much more romantic to have all Reese's attention to herself than to share it with his basketball buddies.

They got some drinks and settled at a small candlelit table with a good view of the dance floor. The DJ played a popular hip-hop song and kids flooded out to get their groove on.

"It's funny how I feel totally comfortable on a soccer field or basketball court, but the dance floor is like a minefield to me," Reese said.

Haley smiled. "And I thought you were good at everything you tried."

"Ha!" He laughed. "Hardly. You know what else makes me totally insecure? Speaking French."

"But you get As in French," Haley said.

"That's because I work really hard at it. And my mother speaks it well and makes me practice with her at home. To speak French well you have to move your mouth in this funny way . . . I feel like a dork whenever I try it."

"You know where I feel awkward?" Haley confided. "Walking through the courtyard at school. With everybody sitting around on benches, eyeballing you and making comments—"

"Oh, I know!" Reese laughed again. "I always dread math class because I have to go through the courtyard to get there, and I feel like all of a sudden I'm walking really stiff, like a robot or something. And then I hear people whispering and I think they're saying *Reese has such a stick up his butt,* or something like that."

"No way," Haley said. "There is no way those thoughts go through Reese Highland's mind. I'm sorry, I refuse to believe it."

"It's true," he said. "I'm a self-conscious, pimple-popping geek like everybody else. I'm Dave Metzger with black hair."

"Oh, please. Now you're really pouring it on. Besides, I don't think I've ever once seen a pimple on your face."

"You just haven't looked hard enough. You're the one with the perfect skin. And you're always so graceful, in whatever you do."

Haley didn't know what to say to that lovely compliment, so she just smiled. The DJ switched gears and played a slow song. Reese stood up.

"Now that I've confessed some of my weaknesses and lowered your expectations, feel like geeking it up on the dance floor with me?"

"Totally." Haley followed him onto the dance floor. He took her in his arms and they swayed back and forth. He was a great dancer and seemed to be completely at ease.

"You're such a liar," she whispered. "You're an amazing dancer."

"It's not me, it's you," he whispered back.

Drew and Cecily slow-danced over toward them. "Break it up, you two," Drew joked.

The music switched to a rock song, but Reese didn't want to stop dancing. "Now I really feel like a weirdo," he said.

"You're not bad for a guy," Haley said. Actually,

he was better than that. He didn't bust any crazy moves, but he could move to the music without looking like a complete spazbot.

They spent the rest of the evening talking, dancing and joking around with their friends. *This is exactly what a prom is supposed to be,* Haley thought happily. *A celebration of high school, friendship and, if you're lucky, romance.* And Haley was feeling very lucky that night. Reese treated her like a princess and a best friend. It was magical.

As the DJ played the last song and the evening began to wind down, Reese leaned in for a kiss. Haley kissed him back, dizzy with the swirl of the dancing and the warm glow of the lights.

"I forgot where I was for a minute there," she said when they came up for air.

"I never forgot who I was with, that's for sure," Reese said. He pressed his forehead against hers. "I know you don't feel ready to get serious with anybody right now," he said quietly. "But I wonder if you'd reconsider. I mean, yes, we're both busy and we're graduating next year, and who knows where we'll go after that. But in the meantime, we could spend that year together, getting to know each other better. Our final year in Hillsdale could be really amazing."

"That's true," she said, sighing. He had a point. A whole year of being Reese's girlfriend sounded like a whole year of wonderful. Why would she want to pass that up just to study harder? Suddenly that decision struck her as wildly foolish.

"You're right," she said. "Maybe it would be okay to get serious with . . . someone." She gave him a teasing smile.

"I hope you mean me," Reese said. "Because if you're talking about another guy, I have to tell you there's no point in getting serious at this stage—you should be studying!"

Sasha and Johnny stopped nearby. "Hey, guys— sorry to interrupt your intense powwow, but are you coming to the afterparty?" Johnny said.

"Spencer rented a whole fleet of limos to take us all into the city for the night," Sasha said. "He's reserved a big hotel suite and stocked it with champagne and everything. You should come!"

"It's going to rock," Johnny said. "But the limos are leaving in a few minutes."

Reese looked at Haley. "What do you want to do? We could go into the city and party, or we could just go back to your place and watch movies in the basement all night. Up to you."

● ● ●

Tough decision. Reese is putting on his best Prince Charming act, but Haley knows that can evaporate in the wrong setting. Can Prince Charming take the act on the road, or will the gritty city turn him into a frog?

What kind of ending does Haley want for her prom night? On the one hand, prom night is for parties, and there's no better place to party than New York City— and with Spencer footing the bill, it's hard to resist. But the other thing prom night is famous for is going all the way—and that's more likely to happen in Haley's basement than in Spencer's presidential suite. One never knows what's going to happen, of course. All you can do is make your best guess.

So what will it be? If you think Haley doesn't want to miss the party of the year in NYC, go to AFTER-PARTY on page 242. If you think Haley doesn't want to spoil Reese's romantic mood and would rather keep the party of two going back at her house, turn to page 239, MOVIE IN THE BASEMENT.

So far Haley's prom night has been magical. Now's not the time to ruin it.

Making the best of a bad situation is all about attitude.

"**T**his can't be the HHH," Matt joked. "Where are the particleboard dividers? Where is the stench of stale roast beef?"

"The prom committee did a great decorating job," Haley said.

Haley and Matt walked into the Grand Ballroom at the Hillsdale Heights Hotel and immediately felt miles away from home—in a good way. Wisely eschewing a theme this year, with a mandate from the juniors and seniors to "just make it cool," the prom committee had simply darkened the ballroom, adorned it with vines and flowers, lit it with candles, glowing lights and warm spotlights and replaced the ceiling with a starry sky. If the room hadn't been full of high school students, they could have been in a garden in the south of France. Sort of.

"Beats our prom by a mile," Matt said. He went to Ridgewood, Hillsdale's rival school. "Not that I'd know firsthand, because I didn't bother showing up. But I heard the post-prom whining. The theme was 'To the Future and Beyond!' and there was this whole kitschy nineteen-fifties outer-space vibe. In what universe is that the future?" He stopped and turned to take Haley in. "Nice dress, by the way. Did I tell you how hot you look tonight?"

"I think you mentioned it." Matt had complimented her several times already, and they were only one hour into the evening. He seemed to think Haley's silver-gray Whitney Klein original dress fit her perfectly, in spite of what Coco had called "pound-adding puckers." He was sporting a classic black tux accessorized with a preppy plaid tie for a dashing, devil-may-care, I-don't-do-black-tie look that was very Matt Graham.

"There's the posse," Matt said, nodding toward a large round table for eight with a front-and-center view of the dance floor. It was already occupied by Coco and Spencer, Cecily and Drew and Sasha and Johnny. Spencer clasped Matt's hand in a bro-shake.

"Dude, glad you could make it. Thanks for dragging his butt in with you, Haley."

Haley smiled. "No problem."

Matt and Haley took the last seats at the table and settled in for a night of partying with their friends. Haley had worried that going to the prom with Matt would be less than fun for her—she didn't know him very well, and what she did know wasn't always so great. Like his buddy Spencer, he was good-looking and knew it, and expected every girl he came across to fall at his feet when he snapped his fingers. Not that that always happened. But he could be sweet, too, and fun to hang with, if a girl set boundaries for him. Haley was determined to draw a line in the sand and not let him cross it.

Haley looked up and spotted Reese and Whitney headed for their table. "Uh-oh," Coco said. "No more room. Whittles isn't going to like that."

"Hey, guys," Whitney said, dragging Reese along with her. "Scooch over and make room for us."

"Sorry, we can't," Coco said. "Why don't you sit there? It's just one table away. You'll be right next door." Coco pointed to the next table over, where Dave Metzger sat with his girlfriend, Annie Armstrong, their friend Hannah Moss and some kind of mechanical robot-looking thing dressed in a tuxedo jacket and sequined cummerbund. Clearly the geek table.

Whitney's face fell. "What? You want me to sit *there*?"

"This is a table for eight, Whit," Coco said. "I told you to get here early."

"But Reese and I went out to dinner, and—"

"It's okay, Whitney," Reese said. "We'll get a table to ourselves. See you guys later." Reese led Whitney away to a table for two in the corner. Whitney kept looking back longingly at her friends. Oh well. Haley had wondered if it would be awkward seeing Reese at the prom with another girl, but at the moment she didn't envy Whitney a bit.

The DJ put on a new dance hit and turned up the volume. "This DJ rocks," Matt said, getting to his feet. "Come on, kids—let's dance."

Their table emptied as he led Haley onto the dance floor and the rest of their friends followed them. Matt jumped and spun and boogied like a dancer in a boy band. Haley was amazed.

"You're a great dancer," she shouted to him over the music. "I never would have suspected."

"My mother forced me to go to dancing lessons in seventh grade," Matt confessed. "I guess it stuck." He grabbed her hand and twirled her around. "Plus I practice in front of the mirror in my room. Don't tell anyone."

Haley laughed. Drew cut in and danced with Haley for a few minutes, then did a funny mirror routine with Matt where he tried to copy every move Matt made. Haley and her friends formed a circle around the two boys as they tried to outdo each other. Matt finally ended up on the floor doing Russian Cossack kicks. Drew tried them and ended up crashing on his butt, to everyone's laughter and applause.

The boys opted out of the next song, so Coco, Cecily, Sasha and Haley all danced together. Whitney ran over to join them. Then Matt jumped back onto the dance floor, saying, "You girls look so sexy I just can't stay away." He took both Haley's hands and swung her exuberantly around.

After an hour of dancing Haley finally took a break and went to the ladies' room. Coco and Sasha were already there, primping in front of the mirror. "I can't believe I'm saying this, but this prom is actually turning out to be fun," Coco said. "I really thought I was too mature for this kind of thing, but if you can get the boys to dance it's kind of a trip."

"Matt's an amazing dancer," Sasha said. "Is he treating you okay, Haley?"

"Fine," Haley said. "We're having a blast."

"Are you guys coming to the afterparty?" Coco asked. Spencer had rented a fleet of limos to take forty of his nearest and dearest into New York City for a blowout in the presidential suite of a fancy hotel. "One of the perks of being the girlfriend of the governor's son," Coco added.

"Or friends with the girlfriend of the governor's son," Sasha commented. "Johnny and I wouldn't miss it."

"I'm not sure what we're doing," Haley said. "Matt said something about getting our own suite somewhere in the city."

"Don't do that," Coco said. "You'll miss all the fun. Unless, of course, you want to be alone with Matt. That's another story."

After a couple more hours of intense dancing and laughing with Matt, Haley wasn't sure what she wanted to do. All her friends were piling into Spencer's stretch limos—including Reese and Whitney.

"We can do whatever you want," Matt told her. "If you're tired and feel like chilling, I've got a comfy suite at the Regency all set up. We can order room service, watch movies, whatever you want."

Coco popped out of the open sunroof of one of the limos and waved to Haley. "Come on, you guys, get in!"

"Or we can party down with the posse," Matt said. "Which could also have its high points. Up to you."

● ● ●

Matt has turned out to be a pleasant surprise: a great dancer and an attentive, fun prom date. Everything is going swimmingly so far. But this is the crucial juncture, make-or-break time. Haley could end the night on a high

note or a low one, depending on what she decides to do next. Does Matt have any more surprises up his sleeve?

If you think Haley has had enough partying for one night and would like a little downtime—and is curious to see what the quiet side of Matt is like—go to page 245, HOTEL SUITE. If you think prom night is for partying with your friends and Haley wouldn't want to miss a glamorous big-city bash, go to page 242, AFTERPARTY.

PROM WITH DEVON

Things look different when you watch them from the outside.

"Lame," Devon said. "I knew it would be lame."

Haley and Devon walked into the Grand Ballroom of the Hillsdale Heights Hotel and looked around at the prom committee's decorations. The ballroom was dimly lit with candles, glowing lights and warm spotlights, and the ceiling had been covered with a blue cloth studded with twinkle lights to make a starry sky. The walls and tables were decorated with vines and flowers.

"What was the theme again?" Haley asked.

"There wasn't a theme," Devon said. "They were supposed to just make it cool. Mission not accomplished."

"It's not so bad," Haley said. "It's better than the gym could ever be."

"Touché." He stopped in the entrance and turned to look at her. "At least one person at this shindig is groovy. That dress is awesome on you."

Haley spun around playfully. "It's a Jack's special. Lots of karma."

Devon looked sharp himself in a charcoal gray skinny suit from the early sixties with a skinny red tie and sunglasses. He took off the shades so that he could see better in the dark ballroom.

"What's Shaun wearing tonight?" Haley asked.

"I don't know," Devon said. "He wouldn't tell me."

"That's not good," Haley said.

They had arrived fashionably late, so the place was already jumping. The dance floor was full of writhing tux-and-gown-clad bodies. Haley spotted Irene and Shaun at a table in the corner. Irene was wearing her fabulous violet tulle dress and Shaun had on a matching purple polyester tux with white shoes and a ski cap.

"Hello," Haley said. "You two look spectacular."

"So do you two," Irene said. She patted Shaun. "All that talk about coming as Bigfoot was just to scare me, apparently. Doesn't he look nice?"

"He looks a lot better than I was afraid he would," Devon said with a laugh.

Haley and Devon sat down. Haley had a feeling Devon was too cool to dance at the prom, and she was right. The same couldn't be said about Shaun, however. He grabbed Irene by the wrist and tugged her up from the table. "Come on, Rini, let's show them how it's done."

"Do we have to?" Irene whined.

But once on the dance floor, Irene looked as though she was having a good time. Shaun was a wild and crazy dancer, veering from the Robot to the Batusi to some odd stomping moves he had to have made up himself. After three songs Irene pleaded thirst and dragged Shaun back to the table.

"Check out the Lipinator." Devon nodded at Ms. Lipsky, a mousy English teacher and prom-night chaperone, awkwardly jerking around on the dance floor with Principal Crum. "How did she ever get Crum to dance?"

Haley made a face. "Is she—is she trying to flirt with him?" Haley couldn't imagine how anyone could find Principal Crum attractive, no matter how desperate they were.

"Ugh," Irene said. "It's like watching wildebeests mate. But oh my God—look at Fatty Matty and Mr. Lyons."

Ms. Matty, a rather hefty school nurse/gym

teacher, was swinging Mr. Lyons, the skinny drama teacher, around like a rag doll.

"That's scary." Shaun wrapped his arms around himself and shuddered as if he were genuinely freaked out. "She's way too butch for him."

"Aw, but look at Travis and his wife," Irene said. "What's her name again?"

"Annabelle," Haley said. Her AP History teacher and soccer coach, the handsome Travis Tygert, had brought his wife to help him chaperone, and they almost looked like a prom king and queen as they danced close together, even though the DJ was playing a fast song. They'd been high school sweethearts. Haley sighed. She hoped she could have a long-lasting romance like that one day.

"I notice Mr. Von's not here," Devon said. "Do you think he stayed away because of the rumors?"

"I think he's still on his honeymoon," Haley said. "Otherwise I'm sure he'd be here."

"Yeah, he's brave," Shaun said. "He doesn't care what a bunch of conformo-bots think about him."

They passed the evening making snarky comments about everyone on the dance floor, until finally the DJ announced the last song, a slow dance. Haley tugged on Devon's sleeve. "Come on, Devon. I know you're too cool to dance but this is our last chance. Just one dance at the prom, that's all I ask."

"I look so bad when I dance, Haley," Devon said.

"Really, once you see it you won't respect me anymore."

Haley laughed. "I'll be the judge of that."

"You have to, Devon," Irene said. "It's New Jersey state law."

"Dude, we're totally grooving to this song," Shaun said, dragging Devon to the crowded dance floor.

Shaun clutched Irene in a bear hug, and Devon took Haley in his arms. They swayed to a corny slow song. Haley rested her head on Devon's shoulder. He smelled nice, kind of spicy.

"You're not bad at all," Haley said.

"Now that you know that you're going to try to get me to dance all the time," Devon said. "Well, it's not happening."

"Don't worry, once is enough for me." She closed her eyes and rocked along with the music until it was over. The end of the prom.

"What's next?" Shaun asked. "I'm not ready to stop. I could party all night."

"Whatever Haley wants," Devon said. "Traditionally, aren't we supposed to go down to the shore and stay up all night to watch the sun rise over the ocean?"

"Aw, dude, I'm not driving all the way down there," Shaun said. "We can watch the sun rise at my house."

"I've never been to the shore," Haley said.

"It's kind of cheesy," Devon said. "But in a cool way. It's actually a great place to take pictures."

"Lots of picturesque rot," Irene said.

"I happen to love picturesque rot," Devon said. "Especially when it comes with run-down motels and funny neon signs. What do you say, Haley?"

● ● ●

Devon likes to stay on the edges of things and watch them from the outside—the artist's perspective. Haley can dig that. He may not be the most enthusiastic prom date, but then, prom is kind of a cheesy tradition—why pretend it isn't?

But how to end it? Keep the cheesiness going with a trip to the Jersey Shore? Shaun and Irene refuse to go, so it's a chance for Haley to be alone with Devon, if she wants to be. Or stay in town and hang with Shaun and Irene?

If you think Haley wants to follow New Jersey prom tradition and head for the shore with Devon, turn to page 248, MOTOR COURT. If you think she'd rather party with her friends, turn to page 252, LA DOLCE VITA.

PROM WITH ALEX

Tradition is fine; just don't let it get too stodgy.

"Nice," Alex said, looking around the Grand Ballroom at the Hillsdale Heights Hotel. "What's the theme?"

"There is no theme this year," Haley said. "The prom committee just promised to make it nice."

Haley and Alex walked arm in arm into the darkened ballroom, decorated with vines and flowers and lit with candles and warm spotlights, with a twinkling "starry sky" overhead. Haley was resplendent in her chic black and white strapless from Mimi's, and Alex looked very grown up in his black Brooks Brothers tuxedo.

"In that case, they did a good job," Alex said. "Last year's prom was a fiasco. This looks fairly sane."

Haley glanced around the room in search of some of her friends, but before she found them Alex pointed to a table at the back and said, "There's Dean and Cassie. Looks like they saved us a seat."

Haley followed Alex to a table full of seniors she didn't know. Alex introduced her: Dean Shapiro, Cassie Clark, Mallory Logan and Josh Meyer.

"I can't believe this is our last prom," Cassie said.

"Everything is our last everything now," Dean said, putting an arm around Cassie's shoulders. "Soon it will be our last lunch in the cafeteria, our last sunny day in the courtyard, our last gym class—"

"—the last time Principal Crum calls an assembly to tear us a new one," Josh cut in. Everybody laughed.

"And then our last summer as kids, really, and we're off to college," Mallory said.

"Where are you all going?" Haley asked.

"Brandeis," Josh said.

"Dartmouth," Dean said.

"Chicago," Cassie said.

"Vanderbilt," Mallory said.

"Wow," Haley said. "Those are all great schools." It figured Alex's friends would all be super-brains.

"I got into Princeton but there was no way I was staying that close to home," Dean said.

"Where are you applying, Haley?" Mallory asked.

"I'm not sure yet," Haley said.

"Maybe you want to follow Alex to George-town?" Cassie said.

Haley glanced at Alex. "I wouldn't complain," he said.

"We'll see," Haley said. "First I'd have to get accepted."

"You would," Alex said. To his friends he added, "She may be cute but she's supersmart."

That comment brought the conversation to a dead halt. Cassie broke the silence. "Mallory, what are you going to wear under your graduation gown? Is it worth wearing a dress and heels or should we change after the ceremony?"

"I think you should go naked under there," Josh said.

"We all should!" Dean said.

"Oh, come on," Mallory said. "You guys would never do something like that."

While the seniors discussed graduation day protocol, Haley's eyes swept the room. She saw Coco and her crowd whooping it up at a front-and-center table, making sure all eyes were on them. She spotted Shaun, Irene and Devon slumping moodily at a corner table, watching the dancers and probably making snarky comments. Then she saw Dave and Annie at a table by the restrooms. Hannah Moss was there with her date, a small boy Haley didn't know. With his curly hair and sharp features, he might have been Hannah's cousin.

"There's Annie and Dave," Haley said to Alex. "I'm going to go say hi."

"Come back soon," Alex said. "We haven't had a dance yet."

"I won't be long," Haley said. She threaded her way through the tables and sat down next to Annie, who was rubbing Dave's knee. "Hey, you guys. Having fun?"

"Yes, very much," Dave said. He did look happier than Haley had seen him in a long time.

"This is my cousin Howard." Hannah nodded at her date. *How did I guess?* Haley thought.

"Dave has some great news," Annie reported. "Tell her, Dave."

"My father called today," Dave said, beaming. "He said he feels terrible about what happened last fall when I went looking for him. He's sorry he rejected me and wants me to give him another chance."

"Isn't that great?" Annie said. "They're getting together for lunch next week."

"Dave, that's fantastic!" Haley said.

"I felt so happy about it, I even decided to forgive Mr. Von for marrying Mom," Dave said. "And I confessed to Principal Crum that I was behind all those rumors about him. They're closing the investigation and his job is safe."

"Good for you," Haley said. "That took guts."

"I still think those films he made were sleazy," Dave said. "But Hannah explained to me that they're art, not porn. And that people shouldn't have their youthful follies held against them forever."

"*Hannah* explained that to you?" Haley was surprised. Hannah was a genius, but not when it came to art, porn or human relationships.

"What?" Hannah said. "It's perfectly obvious."

"And now that my real dad is coming back into my life, I don't need RoBro! so much anymore," Dave said.

"So he put him away—thank goodness," Annie said.

"I made sure he's comfortable, with plenty of blankets," Dave said.

Annie rolled her eyes, but she gave Dave an encouraging squeeze at the same time.

"You two seem pretty tight," Haley said.

"We're in love again," Annie said. "I just couldn't compete with RoBro! I tried to be supportive about him but he was driving me crazy."

"A real human girlfriend is a lot better company than a mechanical brother," Dave said, sounding as if he were reciting something a therapist had told him. "I should have seen that earlier, but I was afraid of human relationships after my father hurt me so badly."

"That makes sense," Haley said.

Alex appeared behind her and put his hand on her shoulder. "Mind if I take Haley away for a while? I feel like dancing with my beautiful prom date."

"Go ahead," Annie said. "Dave, do you feel like dancing?"

"Annie, you know you don't want that," Dave said.

"Dave's the spazziest dancer ever," Hannah said.

Haley followed Alex to the dance floor. They started rocking out to a fast song, but the next song was slow. Alex took her in his arms.

"I'm having a wonderful time," he said.

"Me too," Haley said.

"We can make it last all night," Alex said. "Feel like a drive into the city? Or maybe just a cruise around town?"

● ● ●

Haley's a good sport about hanging at Alex's senior table rather than spending prom night surrounded by her friends. But some time alone with Alex might make up for that. If you think Haley would like to drive into New York with Alex and explore the late-night city life, turn to page 256, SUNRISE IN THE CITY. If you think she'd prefer to stay closer to home, go to page 260, STEAMY WINDOWS.

MOVIE IN THE BASEMENT

When you're with the right person, nothing can make it wrong.

"Wow, two minutes to midnight." Perry Miller opened the door for Haley and Reese as they returned from the prom. "I don't believe it—you actually made it home by your curfew on prom night."

"We aim to please," Reese said.

"Well, you certainly pleased me," Joan said. "We're going to bed, but feel free to stay up as long as you like, kids. Just don't make too much noise—I don't want Mitchell to wake up."

"We'll be quiet as mice," Haley promised. "We're just going to watch a movie."

Haley popped popcorn and put some soda and glasses on a tray. She took them downstairs to the basement, where Reese was flipping through channels looking for a good movie.

"How about *Sleepless in Seattle*?" he asked.

"I've seen it a million times," Haley said. "But I can always watch it again."

She settled down on the couch next to Reese. He pulled a blanket over the two of them. It was a little chilly in the basement on a cool early-summer night.

As the opening credits rolled, Reese turned his face toward Haley and stared into her eyes. They sat like that, nose to nose, for a second. Then, with the slightest movement, he leaned in and kissed her gently on the mouth.

Haley pressed against him, and they were off. They kissed passionately through most of the movie. By the time Haley came up for air, her hair was a tangled mess, her dress was on the floor and the final credits were rolling.

"Mmmm . . ." Reese snuggled against her, rubbing his face in her neck. "You smell so good." They kissed again, and then Reese posed the big question.

"So what do you think? Should we, um, keep going?"

Haley knew exactly what he meant. If they kept

making out at this rate, the next thing they knew they'd be going all the way.

● ● ●

Haley's having a perfect prom night with Reese so far. So what would be the best way to cap it off? If you think Haley should tell Reese she wants to GO ALL THE WAY, turn to page 265. If you think she'd rather save that for later, have her SHOW SOME RESTRAINT on page 263.

A wild party can bring out the beast in anyone.

"Wow, check this place," Haley said as she and the Spencer Eton posse walked into the suite he'd rented at a swank New York hotel. "The Presidential Suite—it's huge!"

"Champagne, a catered buffet . . . Spencer really pulled out all the stops," Sasha said.

"Of course," Coco said. "What do you expect? Spencer does everything first class."

The Presidential Suite had a large bedroom, two bathrooms—one with a Jacuzzi—and a huge living room with a grand piano and panoramic views of Manhattan. Haley sat down on an overstuffed couch with a glass of champagne and a plate of minicrab-cakes.

"Party favors in the bedroom," Spencer announced. "For those who wish to partake." Matt, Johnny and a few other kids followed him in.

"Whew! I'm getting tipsy already," Whitney said, slurping her champagne. "After all the champagne we had in the limo . . . and there seems to be an endless supply here. . . ."

"No worries," Coco said. "We'll all just crash here in the suite. Why not? That way we can party all night long."

"It is prom night," Sasha said. "Partying all night is a prom-night tradition."

Haley glanced at Reese, who was sipping champagne and tinkling the keys on the piano. It seemed as though everybody was up for an all-night party, so she might as well enjoy it. She poured herself another glass of champagne.

Johnny turned on some music and soon people were dancing all over the suite—jumping on the beds, jumping on the chairs, rolling around on the carpet. After an hour or so, all the food was gone but the champagne was still flowing, and everybody was stupid drunk. Haley's head felt pleasantly fuzzy. Matt sat beside her on the floor and started rubbing her back. Even Reese "Natural" Highland, known

243

for his abstemious ways, was roaring drunk. He jumped up on a table with a yelp, tugged his shirt off and started dancing like a male stripper.

"Wow, Reese must really be wasted," Whitney said.

"Yeah," Haley said. "I've never seen him do anything like that before."

"Wait—is he my prom date?" Whitney stared at Haley with unfocused eyes. "Or yours?"

Haley looked at Matt, then Reese, then back at Matt. "You know what? I can't remember."

"Whoa," Whitney said. "Neither one of us can remember who our date is. That's really bad." She started laughing, and Haley laughed too. A little voice way back in her head told her she'd pay for this wild party in the morning. But in the meantime, she sat back and had another glass of champagne. Why not? It was prom night. A night made for memories—not that she'd necessarily remember anything. At least she was having fun forgetting.

THE END

Some guys don't know what they want. They take their cues from the girl they're with.

"**T**his is lovely." Haley surveyed the luxurious hotel suite Matt had rented just for the two of them. "Nice and quiet."

"They've probably already trashed the place at Spencer's party," Matt said. "That kind of wild party is fun, but not very romantic."

"No," Haley said. "Not romantic at all."

She settled on a comfy couch. Matt had arranged for flowers and a bottle of champagne, chilling in an ice bucket, to be waiting for them in the room. He poured her a glass of bubbly.

"Are you hungry?" he said. "We could order room service."

"I'm starving. Must have worked up an appetite with all that dancing." Haley scanned the menu. Matt called downstairs for two club sandwiches with french fries and an ice cream sundae.

"Why don't you get comfortable on the bed?" he said. "We can watch movies while we eat our food, and . . ."

"And?"

"And whatever happens, happens."

Haley kicked off her shoes and went into the bathroom. She changed out of her prom dress and into the hotel's fluffy white robe.

"Is this sexy enough for you?" she joked.

Matt's eyes flashed. "Believe it or not, Haley, you actually rock a bathrobe like nobody's business."

Haley laughed and settled on the bed. There was a knock at the door: room service had arrived. "More champagne?" Matt offered.

● ● ●

Everything's going great so far—but what happens next? Haley has two choices: keep things platonic, or test the romantic waters with Matt.

Will Haley keep her robe on? If you think she should, turn to page 267, PLATONIC PASS-OUT. If you think Haley should guzzle some more champagne and see where that leads her, turn to CALL ME IN THE MORNING on page 269.

MOTOR COURT

There's a fine line between charming and seedy, and Haley knows it when she sees it.

"This is it?" Devon pulled off the beach access road and stopped in front of the office to the Seagull Motel. The Seagull's neon sign was missing the *g* and the *u*. It blinked and buzzed, and a couple of run-down cars occupied a few spots in the half-empty parking lot. It was the cheapest-looking motel Haley had ever seen.

"The Seagull Motel is the pride of Seaside Heights," Devon joked.

"You mean Sleazeside Heights," Haley said,

staring at the strip of liquor stores, dive bars and no-tell motels all around her. A sketchy-looking guy loitered under a streetlight, obviously up to no good.

Devon looked offended. "I'm sorry it's not Spencer Eton's Presidential Suite," he said. "But this is the best I can afford on the money I make working at Jack's. Besides, doesn't it have a certain seedy charm?"

Haley didn't think so, but she could see that this was a big gesture for the usually passive Devon. He clearly thought the Jersey Shore was superromantic in a grubby, Bruce Springsteen's *Greetings from Asbury Park, N.J.* way, so she said, "I see what you mean. Kind of like a scene in an indie movie from the early nineties."

Devon smiled. "In grainy black-and-white. Now you're getting into the spirit."

She and Devon went into the office. A heavyset man wearing a stained white T-shirt and smoking a cigar grunted at them in greeting and gave them the key to room 14. Haley thought she saw a gun on the desk behind the counter. Devon parked the car in front of the room while Haley walked down the breezeway with the key. The early-summer night air was chilly, especially coming off the ocean.

Haley unlocked the door and flicked on the light. The room was small and dingy, with a tattered bedspread, a stained couch and a broken TV. The bathroom was even worse. Under the harsh fluorescent light the sink and tub were coated with a scummy film. Haley tried to suppress her rising nausea. This was where she was going to spend her prom night— in a fleabag motel?

"Not bad, right?" Devon said.

"It's got lots of atmosphere," Haley replied.

Devon took her in his arms and kissed her. Haley could hear someone bumping around in the room next door. "Why don't you change out of that groovy prom frock and into something more comfortable?"

"Okay." Haley returned to the bathroom and shut the door. As she reached back to unzip her dress, the world's largest cockroach skittered across the floor right in front of her. Without thinking, Haley lifted her foot and squished the bug with her new satin pump. Orange goo splattered all over the floor and stained her shoe. Grossed out, Haley let out a loud, girlie scream.

"What's wrong?" Devon knocked on the door. "Are you all right?"

No, I am not all right, Haley thought.

● ● ●

Devon's idea of a romantic prom night is a bit of a letdown, but at least he's trying. Should Haley keep her mouth shut, hang on and try to make the best of it? Or should she tell Devon in no uncertain terms that she

can't take another second in that dump and wants to leave immediately?

If you think Haley would be wise to GO HOME, whether it hurts Devon's feelings or not, turn to page 272. If you think Haley should chill out and stay with Devon, turn to HOOKUP HELL on page 275.

You can follow established traditions, but sometimes it's more fun to make up your own.

"Okay, so we're not going to the shore," Devon said. "That's cool."

Haley, Devon, Shaun and Irene strolled out of the Grand Ballroom, looking for action. The prom was over, there were afterparties to crash, but first, the fountain in front of the Hillsdale Heights Hotel beckoned invitingly.

"If we can't go to the shore, let the shore come to us!" Devon shouted. He jumped into the fountain, suit and all. "Come on in, the water's great!" He splashed Haley and Irene.

"Cowabunga!" Shaun took a running start and leaped into the fountain, windmilling his arms and legs and landing with a soaking splash. Then he climbed out, dripping and looking like the Beast from the Black Lagoon, and chased after Irene.

"You're not leaving this place in dry clothes, Rini," he said. He grabbed her, threw her over his shoulder and dunked her in the fountain.

"No!" Irene cried, but she was laughing.

Devon reached for Haley. "Time for your baptism, Haley Miller."

Shaun raised his arms overhead, preacher-style. "Yes, Sister Haley, come and see the light. Immerse yourself in the healing waters of the HHH and Devon's divine love!"

Haley shrugged, kicked off her shoes, dropped her bag and her wrap onto the sidewalk and jumped into the fountain.

"Hallelujah!" Shaun shouted. "She has seen the light!"

Haley splashed Shaun to make him shut up, and Devon splashed Haley, then Haley splashed Devon back. All four were soaking wet and playing like children in a kiddie pool. Haley tripped and fell against Devon, and the two of them tumbled into the water.

"Hey," Devon said quietly, touching her face. "Water looks awesome on you."

He kissed her, and she kissed him back, and soon they were passionately making out in the fountain while Shaun and Irene wrestled and splashed nearby.

"Woo-hoo! That's one way to end your prom night."

Haley looked up to see the fountain surrounded by Coco, Spencer, Sasha, Johnny, Reese, Whitney, Drew and Cecily, whistling and hooting and cheering them on.

"You'd never catch me doing that," Coco sniffed. "Not in this dress."

"Oh yeah?" Spencer playfully lifted her up in his arms.

"No!" Coco shrieked, kicking her legs in protest.

Spencer swung her light body toward the fountain, pretending to throw her in, but he pulled her back at the last second and lowered her down to her feet.

"Can we get out of here now and go to a real party?" Coco said.

"See you hoodlums around!" Drew shouted, waving as they walked away. Maybe it was possible for their crowds to mix, Haley thought. Maybe everyone could be friends for senior year. Or maybe not.

Shaun splashed water at them and called out, "You're wasting your youth! It's all about the moment! Spontaneity rules!" But Coco and company just laughed and piled into their stretch limo.

"You know what's wrong with that crowd?" Devon said. "They don't know how to have fun."

Haley grinned and kissed him again. "That's right," she said. "Not like us."

THE END

Love can turn the most rigid control freak into a free spirit.

"This place is legendary," Alex said, opening the door to the Blue Note jazz club for Haley. "Every famous jazz artist of the last fifty years has played here. And they're open all night."

Alex wasn't a big drinker, so instead of partying after the prom he'd offered to drive Haley into New York City to prowl the streets and explore the nightlife. Haley was up for anything, so Alex parked his car at a garage in Greenwich Village and started the night crawl with classic jazz.

They slipped onto two empty barstools to listen to the blues quartet onstage. It was one o'clock in the morning and the place was packed. Haley sipped her diet ginger ale and relaxed into the groove of the music.

When the set was over they spilled out onto the buzzing downtown streets. They walked aimlessly, following their whims, looking into shop windows and stopping for pizza. Everything seemed to be open all night and the streets were full of honking cars, taxis and partiers tripping by in sneakers and high heels.

"It's like one big giant prom-night celebration," Haley said.

Alex took her hand. "The city stayed open just for us."

They came to a salsa club. A young couple burst through the door and lively dance music drifted out.

"Let's go dancing!" Haley said.

Alex gave the club a dubious glance. "I don't know how to salsa dance. All those steps and turns and hip shakes . . ."

"Who cares? We'll wing it." Haley tugged him toward the entrance, and Alex didn't put up any serious resistance.

"Tonight is your night, Haley," he said. "Whatever you want to do, we'll do."

"That's what I like to hear." They walked in and found themselves in a huge old ballroom filled with gyrating bodies and a live salsa band onstage. Alex paid the cover charge and took Haley into his arms.

"This is one club we're dressed perfectly for," Haley said, checking out the girls in their flirty, fancy dresses and the guys in their tight pants and shiny shoes. She watched one couple shimmy and spin and tried to copy their moves. Alex gave it his best shot, and though Haley was sure they looked ridiculous, they had a fantastic time. Alex dipped her every time he got the chance, then pulled her all the way up for a kiss.

Before they knew it, it was five a.m. The streets were quieter when they left the salsa club, the nighttime darkness fading to gray.

"What should we do now?" Haley asked.

"I think I know the perfect place to go." Alex took her hand and hailed a taxi. They rode uptown and got out at a fancy hotel. Without a word, Alex led Haley to the penthouse floor. She giggled when the elevator doors opened and she saw they were at the hotel restaurant, which was just opening for the day.

"Two for breakfast, please," Alex said.

The hostess led them to a table on an outdoor terrace facing east. "You'll have the place to yourself this early on a Saturday morning," she said.

They ordered orange juice, cappuccinos and croissants while the clouds lightened over the city. The skyline changed from blue to gray to pink to orange, and finally a brilliant yellow as the sun rose.

"This was the perfect prom night," Haley said. "I can't think of a single way it could have been better."

"Neither can I," Alex said. He brushed a stray strand of auburn hair from her eyes. "Thank you for a night to remember. Forever."

They kissed in the morning sun, pulling apart when the waiter came by to ask if they wanted anything else.

"Here's to a whole summer with you," Alex said, lifting up his juice glass. "And to many, many unsupervised visits at Georgetown."

"I'll be a frequent Amtrak rider," Haley promised, raising her glass to meet his.

"Long-distance relationships aren't easy," Alex said. "But if anyone can make it work, we can."

They kissed again. Haley knew he was right. She and Alex could do anything they put their minds to. And now she'd never been more sure that he was the guy for her, and she the girl for him.

THE END

STEAMY WINDOWS

You're never alone in New Jersey.

On the drive home from the Hillsdale Heights Hotel, Alex pulled over to the side of the road, for safety's sake. He and Haley couldn't keep their hands off each other and were kissing so much he couldn't keep his eyes on the road.

"How's this spot?" He parked by a secluded wooded area, nice and dark.

"Perfect," Haley said. "Just like your lips."

He put their seats back and leaned over to kiss her. Soon he was pressed against her and they were making out so fiercely the windows steamed up. That was when they heard the knocking. At first Haley thought she was imagining it.

"Did you hear something?"

Knock knock knock. "Folks? Everything all right in there?"

Haley and Alex froze. "Police," Alex whispered. He sat up and rolled down the driver-side window. Haley pulled the top of her dress up and tried to neaten her hair.

A policeman peered into the car, shining a flashlight into their faces. "Is there a problem, officer?" Alex asked.

"Sir, would you mind stepping out of the car, please?" the policeman said.

Alex opened the door and stepped out. Haley looked back and saw the cruiser with its flashing lights, a policewoman behind the wheel.

"You kids coming home from the prom?" the policeman asked.

"Yes, sir," Alex replied.

"Have you been drinking?"

"No, sir, I have not," Alex said.

"Are you willing to take a Breathalyzer test?"

"Yes, sir, I am."

Alex blew into a tube while the officer read the results. "Huh," the policeman said. "You weren't lying, kid. That's a first."

"I passed?"

"With flying colors. I can't ever remember testing a kid on prom night and them not having a trace of alcohol on them."

"There's a first time for everything, sir."

"There sure is. But you two can't park here, so move along. And have a good night."

"Thank you, officer."

Alex got back into the car and started the engine. The police cruiser drove away.

"That cop didn't know who he was dealing with," Haley said with a giggle. "Doesn't he know you always ace every test?"

Alex grinned. "That's right. I'd like to pick up where we left off, but we'd better find someplace more private."

They drove slowly through town until they came to a pull-off overlooking the Hudson River. Amazingly, no one else was parked there.

"This ought to work," Alex said. "Now, where were we?"

They spent the next few hours steaming up the windows again, but this time they weren't interrupted. When they came up for air, the sun was rising over the river. As Haley watched the twinkling lights of the freighters and tugs roll by, she hoped she and Alex had a whole steamy summer ahead of them before he left for college.

THE END

SHOW SOME RESTRAINT

Caution is prudent when the parents are only a staircase away.

Haley was torn: the impulsive part of her really wanted to go all the way with Reese that night. He was so gentle and sweet and so gosh-darn sexy and she felt so at ease with him . . . but the sensible part of her didn't feel comfortable knowing her parents were upstairs and could walk in at any moment.

"I'd love to keep going," she said softly. "But I feel weird here, in my parents' house, with them sleeping right above us. And Mitchell—"

"Say no more," Reese said. "I totally understand.

I'd feel the same way if we were at my house and my parents were home." He pulled the blanket tightly around them. "Besides, I could snuggle with you like this all night."

Haley sighed happily. "Me too." She kissed him. They spent the rest of the night making out—and only making out. But it was hot in its own way. In the morning, Mitchell came downstairs to watch cartoons and found Haley and Reese curled up together on the couch, asleep. And fully dressed. Haley woke up, glad she hadn't gone farther. It had turned out to be a wonderful prom night in its own low-key way.

THE END

GO ALL THE WAY

There's nothing more convenient than a boyfriend who lives next door.

"I'm ready," Haley whispered.

Reese gave her a tentative smile. "Are you sure?"

"Yes," Haley said. "I'm sure."

Reese kissed her softly, then spread the blanket out on the carpet. Haley lay down on her back, and Reese lay beside her. They started kissing, lightly at first, and then with more and more heat. Soon they were rolling around together, their bodies locked in embrace.

It was Reese who slowed things down, deciding

they should keep in mind that Haley's parents were right upstairs. "I'm just so happy you're my girlfriend, I sometimes let us get ahead of ourselves. We've got a whole 'nother year together—all summer, and our senior year—to spend as boyfriend and girlfriend. And after that, who knows? We could end up at the same college. Stranger things have happened."

"I know," she said optimistically. "We have plenty of good times ahead."

Reese kissed Haley on the forehead. Then he kissed her neck. She snuggled closer to him, fighting the urge to sleep, giving herself over to him completely, and knowing they still had all the time in the world.

THE END

PLATONIC PASS-OUT

Sometimes snacks are plenty satisfying.

Haley propped herself against a pile of fluffy pillows on the king-sized hotel bed. Matt sat on the other side, the tray of french fries and club sandwiches between them.

"Let's watch a monster movie," Haley said, flipping through the hotel's movie choices.

Matt looked a little skeptical at first. This wasn't exactly what he'd brought her here for. "*Creatures of the Deep*?" he asked.

"'It Came, It Ate, It Barfed,'" Haley countered, rattling off the tagline.

Matt smiled as they settled in for a cozy night of trashy carbs and trashy movies. Between them Haley and Matt polished off everything they had ordered. By the time the creature had returned to the deep, Haley was feeling full and sleepy. As the next movie started and a ravenous alien arrived and began eating everything in sight, Matt was snoring. Before the hungry alien had a chance to regurgitate all over the planet, Haley was fast asleep.

She woke up the next morning with the sun pouring in through the hotel window. Matt was curled up on the other side of the bed in his bathrobe, the TV still showing old movies.

Haley started cleaning up the empty dishes from room service. Matt stirred, rolled over and smiled at her. "Is my virtue still intact?" he asked.

"As far as I know." Haley went into the bathroom and got ready to take a steamy hot shower. It may not have been the most exciting prom night ever, but she'd enjoyed herself. And most important of all, she had no regrets.

THE END

CALL ME IN THE MORNING

Champagne and good judgment definitely don't go together.

Haley opened her eyes and blinked at the morning sun. Where was she? She sat up and looked around. *Oh, right.* Now she remembered. If only she could forget.

The bed was thoroughly rumpled, the sheets twisted around her bare legs. Her clothes were scattered around the room, prom dress tossed over a chair . . . bottles of champagne and glasses tipped over on the table. She was in the hotel room she'd shared with Matt the night before, apparently alone. No sign of Matt anywhere in the suite.

"Matt?" she called. "Matt?"

Silence.

Her head throbbing, Haley dragged herself out of bed and into the bathroom. She splashed water on her face. It was all coming back to her now. A little too much champagne and the next thing she knew, she and Matt were rolling around on the couch, then the floor, then the bed, going way, way further than Haley had ever planned to . . . but she hadn't gone all the way with him, had she? She struggled to remember. No, she knew she'd stopped him at some point, and he'd been a bad sport about it. Still, Matt knew pretty much all there was to know about Haley Miller's bod right now. She must have passed out, and now . . . where was Matt?

She stumbled into the living room and saw something on the coffee table. She picked it up. It was a note.

Haley—Sorry, had to run. You're out cold, I'm still wide awake, and Spencer's afterparty calls. Give me a buzz when you wake up in the morning. Maybe we can have breakfast? If I'm still around.—Matt

Haley slumped into the nearest chair. Great. Matt lured her into this hotel suite, tried to get as much off her as he could and then was out the door. To Spencer's party. Probably telling everyone there what had happened, how he left Haley passed out in his room. Matt didn't even want to spend the night with her.

Depressed, she dug through her bag and found her phone. She dialed Matt's number just to see what he'd say. It went straight to voice mail. Figured.

She showered and dressed and went down to the lobby to check out. Matt had stuck her with the bill. Awesome dude. Good thing Haley had her emergency credit card with her.

Then it was the sad trudge through the quiet Saturday-morning streets of New York to the dingy, creepy Port Authority to catch a bus back to Hillsdale. Not just a walk of shame, a bus ride of shame. The prom couldn't have had a worse ending for Haley.

THE END

Don't spend the night in a roach-infested dump if you can help it.

Haley heard a bang outside. Then another. She stiffened. Were those . . . gunshots?

"Probably just fireworks," Devon said. "I bet some kids are lighting rockets on the beach."

"Maybe," Haley said. "Or maybe somebody just got shot."

A few minutes later, she heard the sirens. Meanwhile, in the room next to theirs, through paper-thin walls, a woman was yelling in a shrill voice and a man shouted back. There were thumping noises, as if they were shoving each other back and forth.

"Ah, the romance of the streets," Devon said. "It's just like a Springsteen album. You know, *The Wild, the Innocent* . . ."

"I can't stay here," Haley said. "I know you think it's cool in a ratty sort of way, but I just don't feel safe. Do you mind if we just get in the car and go home?"

Devon looked disappointed, but he said, "Sure, Haley. Whatever you want. I'm sorry you don't like it. I guess it is pretty skeevy."

"I just have this feeling we shouldn't spend the night here," Haley said. "It feels dangerous. And even if we stayed, I know I wouldn't sleep a wink. I'd be staring at the door waiting for some homicidal maniac to creep in and ax-murder us or something."

Devon laughed. "Come on, let's get out of here. I like driving at night anyway. The roads are clear, a little music on the radio . . . that can be romantic too."

She kissed him on the cheek. "Thank you."

They dropped off their room key at the office and drove away. Haley breathed easier once they were on the Garden State Parkway leaving Seaside Heights behind them.

They were quiet in the car, listening to soft music on the radio, watching the exits go by. Once in a while Devon put his hand on top of Haley's, as if to warm it up.

At last he pulled up in front of her house. It was four a.m. Her parents had left the porch light on, even though they weren't expecting her until morning.

"Thanks for everything, Devon," Haley said. "All in all it was a great prom night."

"You looked amazing," he said, staring deep into her eyes. "I'm sorry about the motel. I just didn't want to let you go tonight. I—I love you, Haley Miller."

Haley had been feeling sleepy, but this revelation jolted her awake. Devon loved her? These were words she never expected to hear from him, of all people.

"I was afraid I'd hurt your feelings when I didn't like the motel," she said.

"No," he said, "you were right. It's better if we wait. . . ."

Haley leaned across the seat and kissed him. He kissed her back, long and deep. *Who knows,* she thought. *I might be in love with him too. We have a whole summer ahead of us to find out.*

THE END

It bears repeating: don't spend the night in a roach-infested dump if you can help it.

"Calm down, Haley." Devon took her in his arms and kissed her on the forehead. "I'm sorry about the cockroach. This is a special night. I didn't want anything to spoil it."

Next door, through the paper-thin walls, Haley heard angry voices and bumping sounds. What were they doing over there, throwing furniture at each other?

Then, from outside, Haley heard noises—*pop pop*

pop—and almost jumped out of her skin. "Was that gunshots?"

"Nah," Devon said. "It's probably just some kids lighting firecrackers on the beach. Relax."

Haley tried to relax, but a little voice in her head kept saying, *Get out. Now.* The neighborhood was sketchy, the motel scary and weird, but Devon kept kissing her, and she was afraid of hurting his feelings. He obviously thought this Jersey Shore pilgrimage was some kind of sacred romantic ritual.

"We can't leave now. We just got here." Devon steered her over to the bed and took off her shoes. "I'll clean these up so they're good as new."

He went into the bathroom and wiped off the satin pumps with wet toilet paper. He got the cockroach goop off but left a water stain on the satin. The shoes were ruined.

"Sorry," he said, setting the shoes down on the floor. "I tried."

"I know," Haley said.

He took off his suit jacket and tie. "Here. Let me help you get that dress off."

Haley pulled her dress over her head and lay back on the bed. Devon shut off the light and started kissing her more urgently. She closed her eyes and kissed him back, trying to forget where she was, trying to imagine she was anywhere else but in a slimy Jersey Shore motel.

They made out for a while, then Devon,

frustrated, pulled the covers over his head and went to sleep. Haley lay awake, blinking in the green light from the digital alarm clock next to the bed, restless on the scratchy, cheap motel sheets, wondering what kind of germs they had on them. At last she fell asleep, only to wake up a few hours later to the sound of screaming and a crash next door.

Her eyes flew open. The alarm clock flashed 3:33. She reached for Devon in the bed, terrified.

"Get off me!" the woman next door screamed. "Get out of here and leave me alone!"

"I'm not going anywhere!" a man's voice boomed. There was another crash, as if he'd thrown a table against the wall.

"Devon, wake up!" Haley whispered, shaking him.

He stirred and opened his bleary eyes. "What?"

There was another crash next door and more shouting. "Do you hear that?" Haley said. "I want to leave right now."

Devon rolled over and dropped a heavy arm over her chest. "What? Why?"

"Why? I'm terrified, that's why! I'm afraid that couple in there is going to kill each other. How can you sleep through that noise?"

"Oh, please," he muttered. "It's just a couple having a fight. The classic domestic disturbance."

"It sounds like he's beating her up."

"Stuff happens," Devon said. "I hear fights like

this all the time in my neighborhood. Just put a pillow over your head until it stops. You'll be asleep in no time."

Furious, Haley covered her head with the smelly pillow. It didn't help. How could he treat her this way, after they'd gone to the prom together and even hooked up that night? Was he so used to domestic violence that he thought it was normal? What did that say about him?

She threw her pillow across the room. "Devon, I won't stay here. Get up. We've got to go home right now."

Devon sat up grumpily, rubbing his eyes and shaking his head in disbelief. "Are you serious? You want me to drive us home in the middle of the night just because of a little noise?"

"This is more than a little noise," Haley said. "This place isn't safe."

"You're just spoiled," Devon muttered under his breath. "Just another spoiled little bourgeois girl, like all the rest of them. Just like Coco and Whitney and that crowd. Maybe you should have gone to the prom with them instead."

"What?" Haley couldn't believe her ears. Why was he turning on her this way? Was he just grumpy because it was the middle of the night?

"I went to a lot of trouble to plan a romantic prom night for us, and you want to leave," Devon said. "You're an unappreciative, sheltered little girl. What are you going to do when you have to face the real world in a year or two? Go running back to Mommy and Daddy every time you hear a scary noise?"

"That's so unfair—"

But he didn't let her finish. "Oh, that's right, you won't have to face the real world next year. You'll be going to some cushy college, all paid for by your parents. Maybe you'll never have to face reality. You can marry some rich dude and hole up in a fancy house and never leave the air-conditioned perfection of your little world. . . ."

Haley pulled the pillow out from under Devon's head and put it over her face. She couldn't listen to this anymore. Here she was in hookup hell: a filthy dump, far from home, unable to sleep and being lectured by her date about what a spoiled brat she was. How could her prom night have gone so wrong?

THE END

CRUDEN'S COMPLETE CONCORDANCE